GAFFREY'S DREAM

by

M. M. Braswell

WIPF & STOCK · Eugene, Oregon

Resource Publications
A division of Wipf and Stock Publishers
199 W 8th Ave, Suite 3
Eugene, OR 97401

Gaffrey's Dream
By Braswell, M. M.
Copyright©2004 by Braswell, M. M.
ISBN 13: 978-1-5326-5241-7

Publication date 5/29/2018
Previously published by Whiskey Creek Press, 2004

Dedication

Dedicated to our children, Laura, Scott and Matt

Acknowledgment

We would like to thank Publisher Bev Haynes and Executive Editor Jan Janssen for their support. We also want to thank Bustman Higgs for reading the manuscript. We offer a special thanks to Editor Cindy Davis, whose efforts made this a better book, and to Susan Braswell for all her help with revisions.

We would also like to thank Hannah Harris for her help.

Chapter 1

The air was so thick with smoke that it was difficult to breathe or see for more than a few feet. Explosions mixed with screams of dying men and horses. Body parts were lifted up on great geysers of dirt and mud as artillery shells rained death upon Union and Confederate alike.

Captain Frank Gaffrey had no thought of winning the battle. His only thought was of survival. His desperate, frenzied actions were fueled by alternating bursts of adrenaline and fear. Outnumbered and outgunned, Gaffrey tried to protect the shattered remnants of his company as best he could. The fighting raged around him. His lungs burned for air as he shouted orders to the living and dead alike. Minnie balls found their mark time and again with sickening thuds. Private Simmons' body lay mangled, his lifeless eyes staring through the haze at the midday sun. Sergeant Johnson's left knee was a splinter of bone fragments, ligaments and blood. Johnson leaned against an abandoned supply wagon and emptied his revolver into the Blue Coats with fixed bayonets rushing towards him. Freddie, the young drummer boy stood next to his shattered drum, weeping.

To Gaffrey's left and right, cannon balls exploded. Swords and bayonets clashed. Curses and shouts formed an eerie death chant. Everywhere Gaffrey looked, terrified men were engaged in bloody hand-to-hand combat. Gripping his saber in his right hand, he drew and fired his revolver with his left at a Union infantryman poised to bayonet a wounded lieutenant. The bullet found its mark between the man's shoulder blades, and he slumped to a lifeless heap on the ground.

Gaffrey felt the stinging point of a saber slash the left side of his face. Gaffrey quickly brought his own saber up to block the lunging Union officer's sword thrust. The force of the officer's blow knocked him off balance. As Gaffrey fell back across the carcass of a horse, his revolver flew out of his hand. The enemy officer seized the initiative. He lunged forward swinging his saber in a wide sweeping arc. Missing his intended target, he fell on top of Gaffrey, pinning him against the dead horse.

Dazed and bleeding, Gaffrey looked up into a man's face no less desperate and frightened than his own. Scrambling to his feet, the Union officer gripped his sword with both hands and raised the blade high above his head for a final death thrust. In a brief moment of hesitation that often accompanies acts of killing, the Union officer allowed Gaffrey a chance to survive. In that instant, Gaffrey managed to grab the knife he kept hidden in his boot and, propelling himself to a kneeling position, plunged it deep into his assailant's ribcage.

The dying man let out a long, hissing moan and collapsed on top of Gaffrey. Gaffrey heaved the dying officer aside and trembling with exhaustion, regained his footing. As he stumbled toward another wounded comrade, Gaffrey felt himself being lifted into the air on a cloud of mud, dirt, and debris. He didn't hear or feel the explosion immediately. It launched him into the sky above the din of violence and destruction. Gaffrey felt like a bird, above it all—free to fly away, but he began his descent. He wanted to keep flying—far away from the bloody horror below, but it was pulling him back like a giant squirming beast, ready to devour him. As he looked down, he saw what the end of the world might look like, a place of fire and devastation, and unspeakable suffering.

* * * *

Frank Gaffrey woke from the nightmare of his affliction as he often did, his heart beating wildly and drenched in sweat. Lying on his blanket with his horse Liberty nearby, he listened panic-stricken for hostile sounds. During what he had come to call one of his "fits", Gaffrey felt especially vulnerable to attack from Indians and carnivores such as wolves or bears. He never knew exactly when the spells were coming, although the symptoms were usually consistent enough--a throbbing headache and a gradual loss of balance. Gaffrey always tried to find a private place to suffer through the hour or so required for each episode.

Gaffrey looked up at the stars. It was still several hours until daylight. The worst of it was over. This spell was no worse or better than the others. He removed the thickly padded rawhide-covered stick from between his teeth and gently massaged his jaws. The first fit or spell caught him by surprise about three weeks after recovering from the concussion and wounds he had received in the battle at Antietam. A deep saber slash, shrapnel in his chest and right leg, and a severe concussion had left him in an Army hospital for two months. When he regained consciousness, he'd been blind. During the third week, his sight returned along with the periodic headaches that felt like the explosions on Antietam's battlefield. During that initial experience, Gaffrey had almost bitten this tongue in two. Since then, he kept a short rawhide-covered stick in his saddlebags within easy reach.

So Frank Gaffrey lay there alone, bathed in sweat and fear, with his blanket pulled up under his chin, haunted by demons from his past and longing for a comfort that eluded him.

Chapter 2

Morning finally came. A crisp, cool breeze blew in from the north as the sun peeked over the horizon. Gaffrey squatted on his heels by the small campfire, taking in its warmth as best as he could. He cradled his old, tin coffee cup in his hands and smiled to himself as he recalled what an old friend once said about his coffee, "Frank, your coffee's strong enough to wake the dead." Yeah, Tom had been a good friend, but like many of his friends, Tom had died in the war. Gaffrey didn't want to remember, but deep down he knew he would never be able to forget. He turned his gaze back to his coffee—hot and strong, just the way he liked it. For a long time Gaffrey had dreamed of a special place where he could feel at home in his surroundings and within himself as well. Sipping his coffee, he felt like he had found his dream. In his mind's eye he had always known that a valley such as this existed. After years of wandering he had finally found the place to make a stand with what was left of his life.

The valley was about a mile wide and five miles in length. A stream crept aimlessly down its middle and the buffalo and bluegrass were plentiful, rich and green-blue. The valley was ablaze with the colors of blooming wild flowers. The bright red Indian paintbrush and the white and purple heather painted a patchwork of color across the landscape. Gaffrey felt that there was nothing quite like the beauty of a summer morning in Montana. It was hard not to feel good in such a place.

Swallowing the last of his coffee, Gaffrey put out his breakfast fire and cleared camp. When he was finished, he erased all traces of his presence. Gaffrey had learned to be a cautious man. In Shoshoni, Kiowa and Nez Perce' country a man had to be both careful and lucky if he wanted to keep his hair. He saddled Liberty and headed into the valley.

Liberty had been with Gaffrey through the war. They were old friends and perhaps in some ways, the best of friends. Liberty was a mountain bred mustang with a deep tan color that blended easily with the mountainside. The mustang's speed and courage had saved Gaffrey's life on more than one occasion.

Gaffrey spent the morning scouting the valley for a suitable cabin site. Midway along the valley he spotted a rock shelf that backed up into the mountain's side. The site had an open field of fire in all directions and could be easily defended. A clear, cold mountain stream curled and lapped along the rock shelf, joining a larger stream in the middle of the valley. Upon closer inspection, Gaffrey also discovered a partially hidden cave. A quick look indicated it should prove to be comfortable as temporary quarters until his cabin was completed. He would explore its interior more fully when he returned with tools and supplies.

Gaffrey dismounted and pulled an old briar pipe from his saddlebags. Filling it with tobacco from a leather pouch, he tamped it carefully with the heel of his pocketknife and lit it, savoring the aromatic smell. Slowly, he walked around the location that was to be his home. Satisfied, he sat on a small boulder and took in the surroundings with all his senses. It felt right. He could feel safe here. After several hours of sitting and watching, Gaffrey knocked out the remaining ash from his pipe. He knew that he had much to do before the winter snows came.

He spent the rest of the day scouting the valley, exploring streams, trails and hunting grounds. Wild game was plentiful. There were also thick stands of ponderosa pine, spruce, fir, and lodge pole pine that would provide materials for a cabin and barn, sturdy enough to protect man and animal from the harsh Montana winters.

It was a magnificent land. The snowy peaks of the Rocky and Bearpaw Mountains stood majestic in the afternoon sun. Although there was no indication on the hard-packed ground that a shod horse had been in the valley in a long time, Gaffrey did come upon some huge bear prints. Judging by the size, the grizzly that left them would weigh over fifteen hundred pounds. A grizzly that large was uncommon, almost unheard of, but the prints provided their own evidence. Gaffrey sat quietly, warming himself on a rock outcropping, surveying his surroundings and pausing to listen as Liberty stamped impatiently.

It was time to settle down. At thirty-four, Gaffrey wanted a home, a place to belong. The peaceful valley was a long way from the fighting he had done as a Captain in the Confederate Army. The year was 1869, four years after the war, but the pain and suffering remained alive in his memory. Antietam still haunted his dreams and sleep with the sounds of dying.

Gaffrey's Dream

The War had divided a nation as well as Gaffrey's family. He was from Kentucky, a border state. His brother, Joseph, fought and died as a Union soldier while Gaffrey had fought under the Confederate banner. He never returned to his home state. His parents had died several years earlier so he felt he had no reason to return. Since the war, Gaffrey had wandered from one place and job to another, unable to find any real peace or sense of belonging. The ghosts of Antietam and the war always followed him. Yet here in this beautiful Montana valley he was beginning to once again feel a murmur of hope. Maybe here he could finally put those ghosts to rest.

Gaffrey had become so immersed in his exploration of the valley he had lost track of time. The falling shadows of dusk and the chill of the coming night prompted him to nose his horse in the direction of camp. It had been a good day, one of the best he had experienced in a long time.

Gaffrey returned to his campsite near a small valley stream. He ground hitched his horse and built a small supper fire with dried wood which would give off little or no smoke. He chewed each bite of the thick slab of fried bacon slowly, licking the salt and grease from his fingers as he ate. Bacon drippings flavored the pone of pan fried cornbread. He sopped the last of the grease with a chunk of cornbread and popped it in his mouth with relish. He sipped the strong chicory coffee slowly, enjoying the remnants of his meal and the moment. When he finished his coffee and cleared the campsite, Gaffrey mounted Liberty and rode back to the cave he'd discovered. It would be a good place to spend the night. He untied the heavy blanket from his saddle and placed it on thick boughs cut from nearby fir trees. It made a comfortable bed and with Liberty as watchdog, he felt secure. He placed his pistol and a shotgun beside him and lay thinking about the possibilities of the valley: a cabin with a front porch, livestock, and a wife and children. These thoughts drifted in and out of his consciousness as sleep overtook him. He slept well, waking only a few times to listen to the sounds of the night.

Gaffrey awoke beneath a gray-tinged morning sky and built a small, smokeless fire. Today, he would ride into town to file a homestead claim. He finished a quick breakfast of coffee and a piece of cold cornbread from last night's supper. After clearing camp and lighting his pipe, he surveyed the valley with the field glasses issued to him during the war, catching a glimpse of a soaring hawk. He listened to Liberty cropping grass. It was a pleasant sound. He spoke to his horse in low, soothing tones as Liberty snorted in reply. The nearest town was approximately three days ride from the valley. Morristown was a small but growing settlement, consisting of two saloons, a general store, barbershop, blacksmith's shop, livery stable, bathhouse, stockyard and a modest hotel. Located on a key trade route, Morristown also offered the potential for a respectable cattle market and future rail line.

Gaffrey saddled his horse and, for several minutes, listened cautiously. He was tired, but it was a good kind of tired, one that made him feel like he had accomplished something of value. A hot meal and bath along with a bottle of whiskey and a soft bed would make him feel like a new man. Gaffrey smiled to himself. Well, maybe not new, but at least some better. Seven days of trail dust didn't wash off that easy. He rode toward Morristown, letting his friend choose his own pace. Gaffrey instinctively used a variety of land cover as he rode, from a sweeping chestnut tree to the shadow of a cluster of sumac. He changed directions several times to confuse anyone who might have followed him. He checked his back trail carefully, stopping often in the shadows to watch and listen.

There were Indians to think about and outlaws as well. Several times Gaffrey came upon tracks of unshod ponies. It was evident that small groups of Indians were on the move, Kiowa or Shoshoni more than likely. As he got closer to Morristown, Liberty seemed to be in a spirited mood, so Gaffrey let him run. He smiled as Liberty broke into a full gallop. The setting sun painted the horizon shades of red and violet as he rode nearer to his destination.

Chapter 3

Downwind of Morristown, Gaffrey slowed Liberty to an easy pace. He listened to voices and the faint sound of a piano playing. He was amazed at how far a cool evening breeze could carry a town's sounds without any visible signs that the place even existed. Nearing his destination, Gaffrey smelled a mixture of aromas: stabled horses, a stockyard, and evening suppers being prepared on cookstoves that slowly engulfed him. He licked his lips in anticipation of several whiskeys at the saloon and a home-cooked meal at the local hotel or boarding house. A hot bath to cut through several days of trail dust, a shave and maybe even a haircut along with a soft bed for a good night's sleep would also be a welcome change. He pulled Liberty to a halt at the crest of the last hill before town. Below him, the flickering lights beckoned.

The livery was his first stop. Liberty was stripped of gear and rubbed down with hay as Gaffrey carefully attended to his horse's needs. Afterwards, he paid the hostler to put on a feed bag of oats. He stored the rest of his gear in the hostler's shed.

Now it was time for the drink he'd promised himself. Walking toward the Gold Nugget Saloon, Gaffrey surveyed the town's main street and the surrounding area with a cautious glance. He paused at the window of the barbershop, running his hand over the stubble of a seven-day old-beard.

Gaffrey's hair displayed several streaks of premature gray. He had dark eyes, stood about six feet tall and weighed 187 pounds. A four-inch scar drew a subtle white jagged line under the corner of his left eye, compliments of a Union saber thrust. Gaffrey was not exactly a handsome man, but there was something about him that people seemed to notice. He wore a tied down .44 colt and kept another colt tucked into his waistband. A finely honed hunting knife was sheathed to his gun belt. His jeans were trail worn and his brown shirt was faded and encrusted with the dirt and grime of his journey. Gaffrey's weathered, calloused hands bore the mark of long trail drives and years of hard work.

Pausing at the entrance of the saloon, Gaffrey noted its layout. It was fairly typical—a long bar in the middle, accommodating a half dozen or so drinkers. Several of the half dozen tables were occupied with various card games. A stairway to the left appeared to lead to a second level where four or five small rooms opened onto a balcony overlooking the bar below. The raucous laughter coming from them suggested their primary function was to accommodate guests who wanted something more than a drink, card game or friendly conversation. Satisfied, Gaffrey walked through the saloon doors into a room heavy with the smoke of cheap cigars and the smell of even cheaper perfume. These two odors, combined with the smell of just-finished trail drives, offered a distinctive aroma all its own.

A heavyset man in his fifties, wearing a tattered brown derby, sat playing an old piano with surprising skill. As Gaffrey would later find out, this odd-looking fellow, in a world of his own, was also the owner of the Gold Nugget. Sitting next to him on a small table was a large glass half-full of gin. For what it was, the Gold Nugget seemed peaceful enough, no fights, although several people were passed out, or on the verge of it.

Gaffrey moved to the quietest end of the bar which also afforded the most unobstructed view. Taking off his hat, he dusted it against his leg and carefully laid it next to him on the counter.

The bartender shouted from the other end of the bar, "What'll it be mister?"

Gaffrey replied in an even measured tone, "A bottle of whiskey, a glass and a cup of hot coffee, Ma'am."

After servicing a few of her other customers, the bartender brought him his bottle and coffee and offered an observation that several other patrons had also noticed, "Haven't seen you in these parts before Mister, and ain't nobody around here called me 'Ma'am' in a mighty long time. You got a name to go with your manners?"

"Name's Gaffrey."

The bartender, a heavy-set middle-aged woman with poor teeth replied, "Well, my name's Betty." She wore a genuinely friendly smile which gave a hint of the handsome woman she must have been many years back. "What's your line of work?"

Pouring out a glass full of whiskey, Gaffrey paused. "I do a little of this and a little of that. I've worked some cattle."

"Morristown's not a bad place," Betty replied. "It's growing a little. They say we may get a rail line which would be good for the cattle business. It's like any other town. It has its ups and downs—it's good and bad."

Gaffrey responded with a slight nod, but said nothing. Taking the hint, Betty said, "Guess you want to be drinking alone."

Gaffrey's response was short and to the point, "Guess so."

He drank slowly and deliberately. His look was neither one of disinterest nor curiosity. It was a nondescript look, one that while accommodating enough, revealed little of what he was actually thinking.

Betty, speaking as much to herself as to anyone else, muttered, "Speaking of ups and downs, here comes one of the downs."

Chapter 4

A large young man, who appeared to be in his midtwenties, swaggered through the batwing doors. He was accompanied by two ranch-hands, who from the way they wore their low slung holsters, were probably hired guns. The brash young man was apparently their leader, or employer.

As he walked toward the bar, the customer to Gaffrey's right spoke in a low, sarcastic tone, "That's Slade Burroughs. He and his daddy own a lot of Morristown. They think they own it all."

That said, the man who had just spoken picked up what was left of his beer and moved away from the end of the bar to a nearby table. In fact, Gaffrey noticed that everyone seemed to clear out from that end of the bar, while people at the other end carried on with business as usual. Gaffrey wasn't sure what it meant, but he was sure that whatever it was, it wasn't good. He slowly refilled his glass. It wasn't very good whiskey, not like the smooth bourbon he remembered from Kentucky. This burned raw going down. But it did cut through the thick Montana trail dust in his throat, and he was grateful for that.

Burroughs and his two lackeys ambled over to the spot where Gaffrey was drinking. Gaffrey looked across the counter at the flyspecked mirror behind the bar. Burroughs had stopped to his right. Gaffrey gazed up at the imposing physical specimen wearing a fancy black suit. An expensive black Stetson was cocked slightly atop his head. He wore a gray suede vest over his fancy white shirt topped off with a silver string tie. Gaffrey rolled his eyes down the 6'4" frame, guessing Slade Burroughs' weight at about 250 pounds. His black boots were polished to a high gloss. His hand-tooled black leather holster held two six shooters with fancy carved handgrips. Burroughs had a broad face with small, cruel eyes. His crooked nose suggested he had been a participant in more than one barroom brawl. This big man was used to having things his way.

"You're drinking at my spot."

Betty laughed nervously. "Slade, this ain't no church pew with reserved seats, this is a bar. There's plenty of room for everybody."

"That's right Betty. There is room for everybody, but not at my spot."

Turning again to Gaffrey, he said, "Mister, I'm talking to you." As if on cue, his two associates moved slowly forward and to Gaffrey's left. Gaffrey deliberately turned to face his adversary. All other eyes in the saloon were focused on Gaffrey and Burroughs.

Mr. Ed, with a weary look in his bloodshot eyes, finished the last of his gin. There was no other sound except for the creaking of a wagon as it passed the saloon. Gaffrey said nothing, but simply stared at the hulk of a man before him. There was a faraway, indifferent look in Gaffrey's eyes that seemed to unsettle Burroughs. As unsettling as the deadness of Gaffrey's gaze was, Burroughs was well aware of the audience to which he was playing. His authority and reputation were at stake and he wasn't about to back down. Besides, he had Slim and Darcy with him, two of his best guns. This stranger might be better than most of the yahoos in this town, but he wouldn't be fool enough to take on three armed men.

Burroughs narrowed his eyes and smiled his most menacing smile. "Mister, you better finish that drink mighty fast because I'm going to drink at my spot with my friends, and my spot is where you're standing. You can either leave on your own steam or you can be carried out feet first."

Gaffrey had seen his type before. The Slade Burroughs of the world came in all shapes and sizes. He'd seen him in a pompous Major during the war, who could barely ride a horse, much less lead a company of men in battle; a Major who had bought his commission and hadn't even made it through his first battle. Parades and ballroom dancing were one thing, but the sounds and screams of the dying were something else. After wetting his pants at the first sound of gunfire, the proud Major had fled from the scene of battle and abandoned his men. He was lucky to avoid a hanging, but since money talks, he was able to buy his way back into a reserve unit with his rank of Major intact. He probably went back to Richmond and bragged about his courageous exploits on the battlefront. Yeah, Gaffrey had seen the face of Slade Burroughs before. And as long as the Burroughs of the world had money and could surround themselves with thugs and halfwits, who would do anything for a dollar and a bottle of cheap whiskey, they would go on having their way. Left on their own they didn't fare too well. He had experienced a bellyful of the Slade Burroughs of this world.

Gaffrey was tired. He loved the land he had found, but knew Burroughs was like a growling dog, which might also bite. He couldn't wait for that type of animal to strike first.

He had to go ahead and make his point even if it cost him.

Gaffrey didn't reply to Burroughs' second warning. He simply looked straight ahead and continued drinking.

Suddenly, Darcy, the larger of the two ranch-hands, lunged forward and grabbed Gaffrey by his shoulders. Darcy was big, but slow. As he reached for Gaffrey, Gaffrey's left hand shot out in a blur and grabbed Darcy by the neck, choking the wind from him and bringing him to his knees. Sputtering and red-faced, his eyes bulging, Darcy tried to wrest Gaffrey's steel-like grip from his neck, but resistance proved futile. Gaffrey responded by tightening his grip. In the same sudden motion as his left hand throttled a surprised Darcy, Gaffrey's right hand closed around his colt. He cleared his holster and pointed his pistol at the center of Slade Burroughs' chest before Burroughs or Slim had a chance to react.

Gaffrey calmly looked at Burroughs and Slim. "I'd like to give you two fellas one more chance to reconsider your demands and let me finish my drink in peace."

Burroughs' crimson face displayed both fury and a hint of fear. His hand lay on his holstered gun. He still thought the odds were good at two to one. But his enthusiasm began to wane as he realized he was included in those odds. He wasn't sure. A thin bead of sweat popped out on his forehead as reality set in.

"Mister, you ain't heard the end of this. You had your chance to walk away. Next time we meet will be the last time you draw breath."

Gaffrey continued to gaze at him with a bone-chilling stare. Suddenly, Burroughs turned and huffed out of the saloon, followed by Slim, who looked back over his shoulder as he left. Gaffrey released his choke hold on Darcy, who by now had gone limp and begun to turn a light shade of purple. He fell to the floor, gasping for air.

Gaffrey turned his attention back to his half-empty bottle. After a few moments, Mr. Ed resumed playing, although not as loudly as before. The patrons returned to their drinking and card playing, talking in hushed tones among themselves about the stranger standing down the son of Hart Burroughs. Darcy by now had regained enough of his composure to half crawl and stumble out of the saloon. As before, Gaffrey stayed to himself. Finishing his drink, he threw down four bits on the bar.

Betty stepped forward and touched his arm. "There aren't many men who would stand up to Slade Burroughs and live to tell the story. You made an enemy that won't go away. You better be careful."

Gaffrey looked at Betty with a wry smile. "I figured as much, but thanks for the warning. You wouldn't happen to know where a man could get a hot bath, a hot meal, and a soft bed in this town?"

"Sure," Betty replied. "Mary Simpson's place, two buildings down on the right."

"Thanks," Gaffrey said, as he turned and strode away, carrying his bottle under his left arm.

Gaffrey paused at the saloon door, looking over the street for signs of an ambush. He knew it wasn't likely to happen tonight. Trouble would most likely come later. He imagined Burroughs would fume about what had happened, drink himself into a stupor, and get the illusion of courage that only too much liquor can bring. Burroughs would plot his revenge with his hired hands and wannabe gunslingers agreeing to everything he said. Yes, trouble would come, but not tonight.

Chapter 5

The sign was freshly painted and to the ·point: HOT BATH 10 cents. Under it, an arrow pointed the way down a narrow alley which ran the length of Mary Simpson's hotel and dining room from front to back. Taking another swallow from his half-empty bottle of whiskey, Gaffrey entered the passageway. Ten paces or so from the rear, a medium size canvas tent covered a raised wooden platform. To the left a large kettle of steaming water rested on the coals of an open fire. Pulling back one of the tent's flaps, Gaffrey peered inside. There were six large washtubs complete with a crudely constructed towel and clothes rack next to each. Apparently at this particular hour there were no bathers, nor anyone feeling the need to tend the fire.

Letting the flap drop, Gaffrey walked to the rear of the building. The view through a window next to the back entrance revealed a young woman stirring what appeared to be a large pot of food, probably some kind of stew, on a cook stove. Gaffrey observed the woman's actions. She looked like a Mary Simpson--like someone who was in charge. She appeared to be in her mid to late twenties and although he could tell she had a strong constitution by the way she worked the contents of the pot, there was also a sense of gracefulness in the way she moved. Her auburn hair was tied neatly in a knot at the nape of her neck. She was a slim woman of average height, but with a certain flair about her. Watching her reminded him of another life where romance, not war, made his heart beat faster.

Gaffrey smiled to himself. With that red hair, he bet she could be a handful if something didn't sit well with her. Corking his bottle, Gaffrey rapped loudly on the door.

The sudden noise startled Mary, causing her to drop her ladle in the pot. She jumped backwards to avoid the splattering gravy. She fished it gingerly out with a pair of wooden tongs and walked decisively to the back door where she quickly demonstrated that Gaffrey's hunch regarding her potential for feistiness was more real than imagined.

"Mister, you do not have to knock my door down to get my attention. Now, what exactly do you want?"

"A hot bath ma'am. Sorry I scared you," Gaffrey replied.

Her blue eyes blazed. "You did not scare me. You startled me. There is a difference!"

"All right ma'am, whatever you say. All I want is a bath, a hot meal, and a room for the night, if one is available."

Regaining her composure, Mary continued, "I believe we can arrange that. Will you be wanting the clothes you are wearing washed as well Mister..."

"Name's Gaffrey," he replied. "I don't know about the clothes. My buckskins are stored with the rest of my gear down at the livery stable."

"Tell you what Mr. Gaffrey, we have some spare shirts and trousers left by former boarders. They should fit you just fine until your own clothes are ready for you in the morning, if that's all right with you?"

Gaffrey grinned. "It's all right with me if it's all right with you."

"Good," she said, smiling for the first time.

Mary shouted toward the dining room, "Bessie, we have a bath customer out back!"

"Be right there Miss Simpson, as soon as I finish cleaning these tables off."

Mary Simpson smiled at Gaffrey. "Bessie will be with you shortly. Perhaps I will see you at dinner."

Gaffrey simply tipped his hat, turned and walked toward the bathhouse. He felt Mary's curious gaze before the door closed softly behind him.

Gaffrey sat in one of the empty bathtubs and took a long drink from his bottle. "I may just get me a little shut-eye, while I wait for my bath water."

Bessie appeared and laughed loudly. "Mister, I don't know if you ever had a bath before, but at Miss Mary's we don't wash the customer and his clothes in the same tub at the same time. You can leave your clothes in a pile at the end of the bathtub while I go get you some hot water."

Gaffrey obliged Bessie. Some six hot buckets of water later, he was really beginning to unwind. He could feel the soreness of the day's ride and the tension of his encounter with Burroughs and his hired guns began to leave him.

Bessie approached the side of the tub. "How you doing, Mr. Gaffrey?"

"Fine," Gaffrey replied. "You know, Bessie, you look a lot like someone I met over at the Gold Nugget--a real nice lady by the name of Betty."

Bessie's eyes immediately lit up and her broad, generous

smile revealed several missing teeth as well as several others that were well on their way to being gone. "Betty's my sister. How did you know?"

Squinting at her teeth, Gaffrey replied, "Just a lucky guess."

"Betty's my older sister," she continued. "I also got seven other sisters. All our names start with a 'B'. Mamma said we'd be more alike and a lot closer if all our first names started with the same letter. Besides, B was her favorite letter in the alphabet. You want to hear my other sisters' names?"

"Maybe some other time," Gaffrey responded as he took an extra-long draw from his bottle.

Gaffrey may have unintentionally got Bessie stirred up, but he wasn't about to add fuel to the fire. Bessie took the hint, and leaving his clean change of clothing next to the steaming tub, she reminded him that Miss Simpson preferred that customers enter her dining room from the front rather than from the rear entrance.

The white and blue calico shirt and worn tan britches fit Gaffrey well enough. He shaved and combed his hair. The growling in his stomach told him it was time to sample some home cooking. When Gaffrey walked through the front entrance of Mary Simpson's establishment, he noticed there were no more than two or three people eating. It was late and he just hoped there would be something left for him.

"Well, Mr. Gaffrey, you look like a new man, all clean and scrubbed," Bessie said, walking up to the table. "What would you like for supper?"

"If you'll bring me whatever you have left in the kitchen that's hot, I'll eat it. And I'd like to wash it down with a glass of cool water and a pot of hot coffee."

The meal was delicious—a bowl of beef stew, two thick slices of cured ham, baked apples and sweet potatoes with a half a skillet of cornbread. Gaffrey ate his supper like he did most things, carefully. He savored each mouthful as he slowly worked his way through the meal. Mary paused occasionally to watch him from her vantage spot in the kitchen. She found Gaffrey intriguing. His manners were polite. She wondered where the scar on his face had come from. She felt silly, hiding in the kitchen, spying on him. Yet she was curious about the stranger who had backed Slade Burroughs down. And when she spoke to him at the backdoor of her kitchen, he hadn't reacted like some of the men in Morristown, their leering looks leaving little doubt what was on their minds. Mr. Gaffrey had looked intently into her eyes. It was almost as if he knew what she was thinking. Mary laughed. How could he? She wasn't even sure herself what she was thinking.

"Mr. Gaffrey, would you like some fresh coffee and the last of these teacakes?" Mary offered as she approached Gaffrey's table.

"Thank you Ma'am...that would be nice. Would you like to join me for a cup of coffee?"

"All right," Mary said, pouring herself a cup and accepting the chair Gaffrey offered her.

Their conversation started casually enough, but seemed to take on a life of its own. They sensed in each other a basic decency as well as a deeper sense of loneliness and need. Gaffrey was a man of few words and Mary, a woman of many; each fit where the other wanted. Their attraction to each other was as distinct as it was mutual. They knew it—felt it within the first few moments of their meeting. Bessie watched with amusement from the kitchen. She had never seen Miss Mary this way and it pleased her. When she finished cleaning, she let herself out and locked up, leaving the two deep in thought and conversation.

Suddenly, Mary looked up at the antique clock on the mantel above the fireplace. "It's two o'clock in the morning. Do you know we've been sitting here for over four hours?"

"Guess we have," Gaffrey replied, stretching his arms behind his head.

Mary rose. "As much as I have enjoyed talking to you, I'll pay for it by lunchtime. Hard work and very little sleep will not add up to a very smooth working day."

Gaffrey said nothing in reply. Looking up at Mary, he smiled. For a moment, she got lost in that smile and let her voice trail off into a brief silence. Then as if returning to her senses, she continued although this time in a softer voice, "I'll show you to your room."

Gaffrey followed Mary. She led the way by the light of her coal-oil lamp, up the stairs and past several rooms of snoring boarders, to the last room on the left. Inside, Mary bent to light the lantern next to the bed.

She turned back the bedcover. "I believe you will find this goose-down quilt quite warm on a cool night like this."

Gaffrey stood behind her. He noticed the curve and shape of her body. He began to feel a warmth inside his belly that he had all but forgotten since the war. Gaffrey didn't know whether it was the whiskey he had drunk or Mary's scent of rosewater. Whatever it was, he simply spoke her name.

"Mary."

She quit fluffing the pillow and turned to him. The look in her eyes was steady and deliberate as he reached out and brought her to him. Gaffrey kissed her gently, first on the lips

24

and then on the side of her neck. Mary suddenly pulled away as if she were having second thoughts. Not quite out of reach, she waited for him to pull her back into his embrace. Yet Gaffrey did nothing but look at her, gently touching the back of her hands with his fingertips. She paused for a few moments, then returned to him with the deliberateness her previous gaze had suggested.

Chapter 6

The first streaks of dawn found their way through Mary's bedroom window. She'd left Gaffrey several hours ago while he was sleeping. She lay in her bed waiting for the dawn, excited yet anxious. She wondered what Gaffrey would think about last night. One part of her felt like a schoolgirl falling in love for the first time. Another part felt apprehensive. Did last night mean as much to him as it did to her? Would he be glad to see her at breakfast or would he be embarrassed and distant?

After several moments of doubt, the vulnerable, giving woman of last night gave way to Mary Simpson, the assertive businesswoman who could hold her own with any man. As she dressed, Mary decided what she would do. She would march right up to Gaffrey's room before the others came down to breakfast and set the record straight. He would have to understand that while last night was very special, he would have to court her in a proper way. She was a lady and expected to be treated as such. Mary walked quickly up the stairs and down to the last room on the left. She knocked three times and waited. Hearing no movement, she remembered Gaffrey telling her how tired he was the night before. He must be a sound sleeper. She entered the room quietly and stopped, shocked to find the room empty. She sat on the side of the bed and stared at the wall for a long time. The room they shared last night had held enough warmth and love to set the world dancing. It now felt cold and empty.

Still staring at the wall, Mary gave way to a forlorn laugh. "Who was I fooling? Like my old Mama once said, 'if it seems like it's too good to be true, it probably is'."

She sat there a while longer and then forced herself to get up and make the bed. As she did so, she noticed a note neatly folded on the pillow. With slightly trembling hands she unfolded it and read its contents. Carefully placing the note in her apron pocket, Mary gave the early morning sounds of a new day a half-smile--a look of hope, tinged with uncertainty; a sigh of sadness, sweetened with what still might come to be. As she entered the bustling kitchen no one noticed the tear she deftly wiped away as she greeted Bessie.

The bell rang three times for breakfast.

* * * *

Gaffrey walked out of the hotel into the faint gray light of the coming dawn. Looking up at the window of the room where he had spent the night, he felt both good and bad. He was grateful for the gift of Mary's affection, but he also felt like a coward for leaving the way he had—quietly and quickly in the shadows of the predawn. Where women were concerned, Gaffrey had always felt clumsy with words and good-byes. The note he had left on the bed simply read: *"Thank you, Mary. I hope to see you again. Sincerely, Frank."*

While his and Mary's coming together had been spontaneous and intense, it was also in a strange way, based upon trust. They were both self-sufficient people, who didn't let just anyone into their private worlds. They had been lovers for a night. Gaffrey hoped they would also be friends and who knew where that could lead. Gaffrey took one last look over

27

his shoulder at Mary's place before he made his way down the street to the corral.

In the stable, Liberty greeted Gaffrey with an impatient snort, stamping the ground in anticipation of the journey to come. Gaffrey and Liberty were both anxious to get on with what was sure to be a full day. The morning air was clean and crisp. It felt good to be alive.

The corral had a dozen good horses for sale. Gaffrey looked each one over carefully. He picked out three and dickered at some length with the hostler. He enjoyed horses and he enjoyed trading. The price was a little high, but the horses were good stock. Gaffrey finished saddling Liberty after retrieving the rest of his gear. He strapped it securely in place and mounted Liberty. After paying the hostler, he rode down the street with a cautious eye, looking for telltale signs of Burroughs or his men, his three packhorses trailing behind him.

The General Store was Gaffrey's next stop. The weathered sign read "Zeke Pitts' General Merchandise." A large, odd-looking spotted hound lay in front of the store on the boardwalk. His tail thumped a lively rhythm. As Gaffrey walked past, the dog raised his head and gave a half-hearted growl. Gaffrey smiled. Not much of a watchdog. He learned later that the dog was Pitts' and that his unenthusiastic growl had in earlier years been much more intimidating. His current relatively mild response was the result of several years' worth of accumulated kicks by customers who didn't find his ill manners very amusing.

Gaffrey also noted how a man's dog in one way or another often resembled his owner and Pitts was certainly no exception to the rule. Pitts himself was a man whose parts didn't quite make up a complete whole. He was a tall, thin, stoop-shouldered man, complete with green visor and horn-rimmed glasses perched precariously on a large hawk's beak of a nose. His large ears were attached to a long angular face which was peppered with liver spots, and made his unusual nose seem all the larger.

Yep, Gaffrey thought, like master, like dog.

Pitts spoke in a low nasal whine, "I'm sorry Mr. Riley, I can't give you anymore credit. I simply can't. I have bills to pay."

The man to whom Pitts was talking was a short, powerfully built man with broad shoulders and well-muscled arms. His booming voice could be heard a block away.

"I ain't asking for no damned handout. I've worked all my life. There just ain't no work to be found right now and my family's hungry."

Pitts' face contorted and his whine became shriller.

"Your problems are your problems. I have enough of my own. Not another dime to you."

Riley abruptly turned on his heel and stormed out of the store, almost bowling over Gaffrey and, by the sound of the yelp outside, gave Pitts' hound a swift kick for good measure.

Suddenly realizing a prospective customer was present, Zeke Pitts curled his thin lips into his best attempt at a friendly smile. "May I help you?"

Gaffrey looked the store over as Pitts attempted to make small talk. Gaffrey was impressed with the variety and quality of the goods for sale. The store had an ample selection of food, clothing, tools, house-ware items, guns, ammunition, and saddlery. It soon became obvious that Pitts was a shrewd trader and businessman.

Gaffrey purchased three pairs of jeans and three shirts. He went into a back room and changed into a new suit of clothes. He also purchased a new hat to replace his old sweat-stained one. He bought a heavy winter coat and six wool blankets. His purchase of food supplies was also substantial and included salt-cured slabs of bacon, dried beef jerky, coffee, salt, sugar, flour, dried beans and fruit. He rounded out his food supplies with some new cooking gear and two extra canteens.

Gaffrey knew clearing land, building a cabin, and all that went with it would be hard work so he chose his tools with great care. He purchased three sturdy axes, two broad axes, an adze, one auger, several wedges, and three hundred feet of heavy rope. The last items were tobacco and ammunition. Five pounds of smoking tobacco were stacked on top of boxes containing 200 rounds of .44 cartridges, 400 rounds of rifle cartridges, and a case of twelve-gauge buckshot.

After one last look around the store, Gaffrey seemed satisfied and said to a thrilled Pitts, "I guess I'm ready to settle up."

"Yes Sir," responded the storeowner, as he tallied the bill. Double-checking his figures, he handed the bill to Gaffrey and with an effort to be humorous said, "You sure got a lot of ammunition there Mister. You planning on starting a war?"

Gaffrey remained silent, but his look said it all. He tamped some fresh tobacco in his briar and lit it, as Pitts laughed nervously at nothing in particular. Gaffrey carefully loaded his supplies onto the packhorses.

After filing his land claim, Gaffrey had one last purchase in mind. At the Gold Nugget, he bought four bottles of whiskey to take the chill off the winter nights to come. As he paid for the whiskey and said his goodbyes to Bessie, he noticed the man named Riley from the General Store. He sat alone at a table in the nearly empty saloon. He was nursing a half-empty mug of beer.

Gaffrey asked Bessie, "What's with that fellow Riley?"

Bessie stopped wiping the rag across the counter and looked at the forlorn man. "Jacob Riley's a good man. Good as they come. He can't find work and his family is in a bad way. He could lose his place across the street and he's getting a mite desperate."

Gaffrey looked away for a moment, lost in thought, before patting Bessie on the hand as a final good-bye. Picking up the whiskey, he walked slowly over to where Jacob was sat.

Looking down at the brooding Riley, Gaffrey said, "You looking for work?"

Jacob looked up with a weary mixture of suspicion and a dash of hope. "I'm willing to work, if you're willing to pay."

"I could use a good hand to help me build a cabin and clear some valley land. I'll pay you twenty dollars a month and furnish the food."

Jacob's features softened somewhat when he realized Gaffrey was serious. He extended his hand and said, "I'll take the job Mister, name's Jacob Riley."

With a handshake the deal was done. A man's word was his bond in those days. If a man's word was not any good, it didn't take people long to know it.

Gaffrey gave Jacob two months pay in advance and a note for credit at Zeke Pitts' General Store—enough to pay his debts and to take care of his wife and children through the winter. Jacob's look of gratitude was clear when Gaffrey handed him the money. Gaffrey had given him his dignity back and in return, Jacob would become a trusted and loyal friend.

After a tearful good-bye between Jacob and his family, the two new friends began their journey to the place where Gaffrey hoped his dream would become a reality.

Chapter 7

Gaffrey and Jacob rode out of town with the packhorses trailing.

"We won't make the valley by sundown, but we'll get a good start," Gaffrey said as he lit his pipe. He was glad to be on the trail. He preferred the wide-open spaces, places filled with rivers, lakes, rolling hills and snow-capped mountains. The day held forth a clear, blue sky without a cloud in sight. Jacob chewed deliberately on a piece of beef jerky as they rode. Each man for the most part kept his thoughts to himself, yet each had his own special dreams. With the beginning of such a beautiful new day, hope ran strong.

After several hours on the trail, despite his best efforts to shake it, an increasing sense of foreboding began to surround Gaffrey. While he always tried to plan ahead and carefully think through his course of action, he was by nature more intuitive than analytical. He felt trouble coming as surely as he felt the chill of an early Montana morning. During the war, Gaffrey's survival instincts honed themselves to an acuteness similar to that of a wild animal. By now, it was second nature. He watched with all his senses without making a conscious decision to do so.

They rode at a moderate, even pace, using all available

cover. The only sounds were those of the horses and occasional squeaking of saddle leather. White men or red men, danger was always a possibility in this country. A wry smile found its way to Gaffrey's face as he considered how a place so beautiful and peaceful could at the same time be so wild and unpredictable. Jacob wore his six-shooter like he knew how to use it. Gaffrey hoped so. If the tight feeling in his gut were any indication, he would need Jacob Riley for more than cabin construction. He really did not know very much about Jacob the man, but he had a good feeling about him. He hoped he was the man he appeared to be.

After stopping briefly to water the horses, Gaffrey and Jacob resumed their journey. An hour back on the trail, Gaffrey's neck began to tighten along with the knot in his gut. He quietly checked the two scabbards attached to his saddle. One held a Henry rifle and the other his sawed-off, double-barreled shotgun. Gaffrey pulled the shotgun from its scabbard and loaded it with buckshot as he rode. Gaffrey hung it over his right shoulder, with the barrels pointing down. If someone were looking at Gaffrey as he approached, the only part of the shotgun that would be visible was the rawhide strap.

Jacob broke the silence, "What's the matter, you 'spectin' trouble?"

Gaffrey recounted the confrontation with Slade Burroughs the previous night.

"I'd done heard 'bout you makin' a fool out of Burroughs—you'd a done the town a favor if you'd killed him." Jacob emphasized his opinion by spitting a straight line of tobacco juice at the bleached skull of an unlucky steer.

The men rode the rest of morning without any sign of trouble. They stopped at noontime for a brief rest. Jacob fried bacon and bread and made a pot of strong coffee. The horses cropped grass as the two men ate in silence. When the meal was finished, Gaffrey and Jacob returned to the trail once more. There was little evidence that anyone had passed that way recently.

Gaffrey led off at a brisk pace, letting Liberty choose his speed. A drove of ducks from a nearby watering hole lifted high into a cloudless sky. Soon, the trail entered a narrow canyon. The mouth of the canyon was about thirty feet wide and remained narrow for about two hundred yards. The canyon then made an abrupt turn west. Gaffrey and Jacob rode without speaking, maintaining as clear a field of vision as possible. The canyon's width decreased after its westward turn. The area now narrowed to approximately one hundred feet at the widest point.

They rode in single file with searching eyes. The rocky canyon walls weren't more than twenty feet high at any given point. Barren rock formations with their shadowed nooks and corners hid more than they revealed. They seemed dark and foreboding in contrast to the bright sky above them.

The knot in Gaffrey's gut grew tighter as he watched Jacob drink deeply from his canteen. Gaffrey took off his hat and wiped his forehead with the back of his hand. As they rounded the turn to his left, Liberty began to snort and stamp. Trouble was near. A sharp intake of Jacob's breath caused Gaffrey to peer into the shadows ahead of them.

Less than one hundred feet away sat the imposing figure of Slade Burroughs astride a large painted mount. Burroughs hands, Slim and Darcy, were on his left and two other gunhands were positioned to his right. Burroughs balanced the barrel of a Winchester in the crook of his left arm. Darcy held his six shooter in his right hand, which was draped across his saddle pommel. Slim and the other two men aimed their rifles directly at Gaffrey.

The knot in Gaffrey's gut began to move up to his throat.

Darcy cocked his pistol. The only one who didn't move was Slade Burroughs. Gaffrey touched the barrel of his shotgun, swallowing his fear and considering Slade's next move. Burroughs would want to make a speech before the shooting started. His kind always did. First humiliate, then kill.

Chapter 8

"Been expecting you, Mr. Gaffrey," Burroughs shouted.

Jacob Riley swore under his breath. He was directly behind Gaffrey and could not shoot at Burroughs or his men without endangering his companion. Gaffrey, for all practical purposes, was on his own. The only element in his favor was that the five men were bunched together because of the narrow canyon.

Gaffrey confirmed his assessment of the situation. As with all bullies, Burroughs would want to intimidate him and Jacob before the shooting started. If Burroughs had placed his gunmen along the top of the canyon, they could have shot Gaffrey and Jacob out of their saddles with no difficulty. But then Burroughs was no military strategist. With plenty of money provided by a doting father, Burroughs had always been able to buy enough loyalty to have his way in most any situation. Yes, Slade Burroughs intended to strike fear by his presence with four gunmen. He would want to bluster awhile before pulling the trigger. To Burroughs, humiliating Gaffrey was just as important as killing him. Without the humiliation, the act of killing would bring little pleasure.

Gaffrey seemed calm, almost relaxed—as if he didn't care one way or the other. It gave Burroughs the same uneasy feeling he had previously experienced in the saloon encounter. But this time he was prepared.

"You'll die in this canyon. And your friend as well," Burroughs shouted. "I'm going to finish what you started at the Gold Nugget. The buzzards will pick your bones clean."

Burroughs waited for a response, but Gaffrey's face wore no expression nor did his blank stare show any emotion. Then Gaffrey did an unusual thing; he took the top off his canteen and took a long drink from it. The other gunmen responded by cocking their weapons, but Burroughs gave no order to commence firing, stubbornly waiting for Gaffrey's plea for mercy.

After he finished his drink, Gaffrey held his canteen at arm's length in his left hand. Turning it upside down, he emptied the remaining water on the ground. The Indian pattern on the sides of the canteen was clearly visible in the bright sunlight. All eyes, including Jacob's, focused on the water pouring from the canteen in a moment's confusion and a moment was all that was needed.

Gaffrey threw the canteen straight up in the air and the eyes of Jacob, Burroughs, and the gunmen followed its path reflexively. In a split-second, Gaffrey dug his spurs hard into Liberty and rein-snatched the horse to his immediate left. With a single motion, he dropped his right shoulder and rotated his shotgun into a firing position as Liberty lurched to his left. A shot burned his right shoulder as he turned. The horse's speed and obedience to his sudden command was the only thing that saved Gaffrey's life. Another shot passed within an inch of his face, taking his breath away.

Gaffrey pulled both triggers of his shotgun at once, throwing two barrels of buckshot into Burroughs and his gunmen. Horses screamed. Men cursed. Gaffrey was again on the battlefield. In a single fluid motion, he dropped his shotgun and emptied his Colt into what was left of the gunmen. In a matter of seconds it was over.

For Gaffrey, like many men who survived the battles of war, there was an order to his choice of targets. He fired at Slade, Darcy and Slim, figuring they would be more dangerous and less likely to spook than the other two gun-hands. The double-barreled blast from the twelve gauge knocked Burroughs and Darcy from their saddles. Their wounded horses ran wildly from the carnage. The buckshot also severed the jugular vein of Slim's horse. The terrified animal reared up on his hind legs, blood spurting from his neck, before collapsing and pinning Slim's legs beneath him. As Gaffrey had expected, the other two gun-hands were confused by the suddenness of his attack. He dropped one of them out of his saddle with a single shot from his colt. The gun-hand fired his rifle wildly into the air as he fell to the ground. Gaffrey shot the other ambusher in the ribcage as the man frantically spurred his horse in an attempt to get away.

Slade Burroughs twitched face down on the ground. Darcy was dead. Slim lay trapped under his lifeless horse. He clutched his shattered and bleeding shoulder. The badly wounded survivor fled in panic, holding precariously to his horse's mane.

"Help me mister. Don't let me die out here," Slim moaned.

Gaffrey looked at the wounded man but didn't respond. He walked to where Burroughs lay and rolled him over on his back. Burroughs' chest was covered with blood. Mucous and blood dribbled from the corners of his mouth. He was lung-shot and labored painfully for each shallow breath.

Burroughs glared at Gaffrey and tried to whisper something. His voice trailed off in a final death gasp, "Damn you."

Burroughs body went limp. His eyes stared upward, seeing nothing.

Gaffrey kneeled and peered intently at Burroughs for several moments before closing the dead man's eyes and saying ever so softly, "I've been damned for a long time. One more won't make much difference."

An echoing report from Jacob's Winchester cut short Gaffrey's moment of reflection. Rising, he saw the lifeless body of Slim, a small derringer clutched in his hand. He offered Jacob his thanks. Jacob said nothing, but tipped his hat and spat a line of tobacco juice in acknowledgment.

Gaffrey could feel the beginning of another headache. The gnawing ache in the back of his skull was beginning its familiar drumbeat. The tiny echo that started between his ears would soon sound like cannon balls.

Gaffrey and Jacob gathered the bodies and tied them across the horses. The wounded horse was too badly injured to save. Jacob's rifle spared it from any further suffering with a single shot. The ride back to Morristown would be a long one.

* * * *

The sun was setting as they rode into town. Gaffrey hitched the horses in front of Sheriff Gene Hill's office. Gaffrey sensed the instant he met him that Sheriff Hill was a no nonsense lawman. He had graying hair and hard gray eyes. His weather worn face had the deep lines of a man who had worked and lived hard all his life. Although the sheriff walked with a slight limp, he stood erect as if he had a ramrod for a spine. Gaffrey felt an instant sense of kinship with Gene Hill. He was a man who meant what he said.

The Sheriff identified the bodies, shaking his head as he did so. Pulling back the tarp that covered them, he bent to examine their faces with a frown, "I knew Slade'd get himself killed sooner or later. He fancied himself a gunslinger of sorts. He fancied himself a lot of things. 'Course the folks in this town didn't much fancy him. Mostly they was scared of him."

"How about you, Sheriff?" Gaffrey asked, taking off his hat and running his hand through his hair.

Sheriff Hill lit the cigarette that he'd been rolling and exhaled a blue spiral of smoke before replying. "Me? I didn't much fancy him either. Me and his old man, Hart, had us several donnybrooks over his boys' actions. But like most towns, this one's no different. Sometimes money talks and justice walks."

Taking another draw off his cigarette, he looked at Gaffrey. "So, tell me what happened, Mister, so I can decide whether to arrest you or let you go."

Gaffrey gave the Sheriff a detailed explanation of the attempted ambush. Tossing his cigarette butt to the ground, Sheriff Hill pulled a toothpick out of his pocket. He chewed on it while Gaffrey talked.

Sheriff Hill looked Gaffrey straight in the eye for several moments after he finished. Then he flipped what was left of his toothpick into the dusty street. "There's gonna be hell to pay. The old man set store by his only son. He was worthless and no account, but he was the man's only child. Yessir, there will be hell to pay."

"I'm hunting no more trouble," Gaffrey replied as he mounted his horse. "Next trip I make for supplies, I'll check in with you."

Sheriff Hill nodded his approval as Gaffrey and Jacob mounted their horses and galloped into the twilight.

Chapter 9

Gaffrey peered through his field glasses into the twilight. He looked again at what appeared to be two mountain men squatting around a campfire. He and Jacob approached the camp, calling out from a safe distance. To ride up to a campfire without a warning could get a man killed. The mountain men whispered briefly. One nodded. The other seemed to disagree, but the first made the decision. He stepped forward and motioned Gaffrey and Jacob into the camp.

Dusk was moving into darkness as they ground-hitched their horses and tied the packhorses to a deadfall.

"Name's Gaffrey. This fellow's Jacob Riley."

The larger man with a scraggly beard motioned Gaffrey and Jacob to come forward. "I'm John Brooks and this here's Wildcat Haynes."

Wildcat poured Gaffrey and Jacob cups of coffee. "You two fellers ridin' from Morristown?" he queried with a toothless grin.

"Yeah," Gaffrey replied.

"Them packhorses look like they got enough provisions to last quite a spell," Wildcat continued, spitting into the fire.

"We got what we need, nothing more," Jacob chimed in, glancing sideways at Gaffrey.

41

He didn't like the way Wildcat was eyeing their supplies. John Brooks took another swig from his jug and wiped his mouth with a grimy, tattered sleeve of his buckskin shirt.

"Where you two fellers headed?"

Gaffrey poked the campfire with a stick. "We plan to scout some land further north," he answered, staring at the hot embers.

Brooks' eyes narrowed slightly. "We been up north. Might be of some help if we knew where you was headed."

Gaffrey looked up from the fire. "We appreciate your offer, but the truth is we aren't sure where we're headed. Just heard from some folks in town that there's some good land still available up north."

Wildcat slurped some more whiskey and broke the silence with a guffaw. "Yessiree, there's shorely some good land north of here. Good for losing your hair to a Kiowa, or your backside to a cougar," Wildcat heehawed again before continuing.

"Or becomin' some fine eatin' for a hungry grizzly. If you ask me, which you ain't, the land up north is good all right-- good for nothing."

"That's right, you tell 'em Wildcat," Brooks added, with a chuckle as he poured Gaffrey and Riley a fresh cup of coffee.

Wildcat was picking up steam, fueled by a belly full of cheap whiskey. "Matter of fact, me an' a full grown cougar tangled in them mountains. He caught me by surprise and got in a few good licks, but once I got my bearings, I made quick work of him. Damn shore did."

As Gaffrey listened to Wildcat's tall tale, he was startled by a strange noise to the left of the campfire. The sounds seemed to come from the area where the trapper's supplies were randomly stacked. He quickly drew his colt and dropped to one knee. Brooks and Haynes looked at Gaffrey, then at each other before roaring with laughter.

"You spook mighty easy, don't you neighbor?" Brooks sputtered between laughs. "And your friend, too. Both you fellers can holster your guns. That ain't no Grizzly over there, just a no-account squaw. She can't hurt you none."

The trappers looked at each other again and the laughter started anew. Both men rolled on the ground holding their sides as they howled. Jacob smiled, but Gaffrey didn't see the humor of it. He could now see more clearly that a young Indian girl lay half concealed in some blankets next to a bundle of furs. He hadn't figured the two men out, but he didn't have a good feeling about them. They seemed like a couple of harmless buffoons, but the small knot that was forming in his stomach suggested otherwise.

Gaffrey carefully observed the two bearded men sitting across from him in flickering firelight. Both were powerfully built and unkempt, Brooks being the older of the two and probably the smarter—if such a possibility existed. He was a large brooding man with thick protruding eyebrows. Wildcat on the other hand, was a full head shorter than his companion. His name apparently came from a scrape with a mountain cougar about which he had been waxing eloquently. To hear him tell it, the cougar was the loser, but from the look of Haynes, it was hard to tell who won and who lost. Several ugly scars ran across his right cheekbone. There was little left of his left ear and the massive scar tissue around his right eye explained why his right eye always seemed to be looking to the left. Earlier, Gaffrey had noticed that Wildcat walked with a pronounced limp—from the looks of it, the result of a poorly set broken leg. Wildcat made Gaffrey uneasy. He seemed harmless, but also unpredictable. Maybe it was the alcohol or maybe the alcohol helped. Whatever the reason, the craziness the wild-eyed trapper had in him came to life. From the look and smell of both men, neither had bothered to take a bath in months. Gaffrey's senses were on full alert.

With some degree of misgiving, Gaffrey and Jacob accepted the trappers' invitation to share their campsite for the night. Midway into the second pot of coffee, Wildcat brought out three fresh jugs of whiskey from the stack of supplies.

He placed one jug between Gaffrey and Jacob.

"You two fellers can share this jug. Me and old John each has to have our own jug—we get mighty thirsty when we have company." With that pronouncement Wildcat turned up his jug and sloshed down a long drink.

Brooks and Wildcat again roared with laughter. In fact, the two of them seemed to laugh at anything and everything, as if they were sharing a private joke. Although Gaffrey found them strange, their tall tales were entertaining enough.

"Damn straight, Big John! That grizzly chased us to the edge of that cliff. I even lost my jug whilst I was runnin' for my life. We had to jump. Didn't have no choice. No-siree. When we hit that icy water below, I thought my heart done stopped."

"At least that cold water sobered us up," Brooks added with a roar.

As the trappers reveled in their exploits, real or imagined, Gaffrey assessed their potential as allies or enemies. In fact, Wildcat Haynes was just finishing a story with quite a flourish. Glancing in the direction of the Indian girl, Gaffrey wondered what would happen to her.

"Why you keep lookin' over at that squaw Mister? You want some o' that?," Wildcat offered with a drunken grin. Rising unsteadily to his feet, he motioned Gaffrey to follow him.

Gaffrey continued to sit cross-legged by the fire. "I appreciate your offer, but I believe your squaw's asleep," Gaffrey replied, hoping to avoid whatever Wildcat had in mind.

Wildcat tossed Gaffrey an incredulous look, took another draw from his jug and chuckled, "Asleep! A squaw's never too tired to do her duty."

Standing over the girl, Haynes jerked off the blanket. He gave her a hard kick which brought little more than a whimper from her. A second kick brought a louder series of moans and groans.

"You ain't too tired to take care of our guests are you?"

Without opening her eyes, as if on cue, the girl wearily pulled up her tattered buckskin skirt.

"Yep, she performs her female duties ever' day to the both of us, whether she's willin' or not—don't she Big John?"

"That's right Wildcat and any man who shares our likker, shares our squaw," Brooks added with a sneer.

He looked at Gaffrey with a menacing grin, "You ain't refusing our hospitality are you Mr. Gaffrey?"

Then suddenly laughing again, Brooks and Haynes took another long draw from their jugs. Both men were obviously drunk and having a good time. Still, there was an undercurrent in their merriment. Raucous laughter and whiskey drinking aside, there was a dangerous edge to their antics.

"Come on Gaffrey, we done told you she ain't no grizzly," Brooks continued.

"Who-ee! That's right!" Wildcat shouted. "We done trained her good. There ain't much left of her, but whatever there is, she'll give it to you."

Gaffrey felt the knot in his gut expanding into his chest. Haynes and Brooks were disgusting. The girl might be an Indian, but she didn't deserve this. They treated their packhorses better.

Gaffrey walked over to where the girl lay, not wanting to confront the trappers, but with no intention of participating in any further abuse of the girl. A closer look revealed the girl's hands were bound tightly by rawhide straps. The lantern that Wildcat brought with him revealed that her wrists were scabbed over and infected. A steady, low moan emanated from the girl as she lay there waiting to do her duty. Her eyes remained closed as if to block what was about to happen and had happened a thousand times before.

Wildcat was again pulling hard on his jug of whiskey. He passed the jug to Brooks who had stumbled over to where the girl lay. Brooks lifted the jug for a long drink and offered it to Gaffrey. He took it and turned it up, trying to buy time as he tried to figure out how to resist any further involvement with the trappers. His earlier shoot-out with Burroughs and his gunmen had left him exhausted. He didn't need anymore trouble, but he was beginning to feel that trouble was getting ready to find him. He needed sleep; his head was beginning to hurt. He didn't want to get involved, but he knew the girl couldn't last much longer the way they were treating her. A part of him would like to just mount up and ride away, but the other part felt a deep anger when he encountered cruelty to human and animal alike. It made him feel responsible in a way that often seemed to bring trouble.

Gaffrey took another draw from the jug. "She looks like she's in pretty bad shape."

"She's our slave, bought an' paid fer," John Brooks replied. "I gave some Kiowas three good hosses fer her. She may be small and sickly, but a few good kicks will bring her back to life!" With that he reeled back and kicked her hard in the ribs.

Brooks grinned, the light from Wildcat's lantern exposed crooked, tobacco stained teeth.

"What would you take for the squaw?" Gaffrey asked disinterestedly as though he were purchasing a new pack mule.

Jacob's eyes widened in surprise. Brooks and Haynes looked at each other, no longer smiling.

"She ain't fer sale at no price," Wildcat replied.

Gaffrey knew the time had come to choose, either let it go or get involved. A quick glance at Jacob, who was squatting next to the campfire, signaled that he had chosen to cross the line. Jacob poured himself a cup of coffee and eased the safety thong off his six shooter.

"You haven't even heard my offer," Gaffrey continued, "I got something that's mighty valuable. It's in my bedroll."

Gaffrey let Wildcat and Brooks try to imagine through their cheap whiskey haze what could possibly be in a bedroll that was valuable.

"You don't say?" Brooks replied, glancing sideways at Wildcat and fingering his beard.

The trappers' suspicions were somewhat tempered by their curiosity. Gaffrey walked to his horse, untied his bedroll and returned with it to where the men were standing.

"What in blazes is so damn valuable 'bout a bedroll?" Wildcat Haynes inquired as he turned the whiskey jug up, drinking sloppily. "I don't see nothin' that makes me want to dance and shout."

With a single motion, Gaffrey pulled out his shotgun, eased both hammers back, and pointed the gun directly at Hayne's face. Brooks, standing several feet to the right and rear of Haynes, was also in the range of the shotgun. As if to add a point of emphasis, both trappers could clearly see that Jacob had risen. He had drawn his six-shooter and taken dead aim at John Brooks. The trappers froze in a state of drunken confusion. The only sounds were those of the crackling fire and the two men's heavy breathing.

Gaffrey broke the silence, "The girl will be coming with us. I'm giving you the price of the horses, which is more than she's worth to you."

"You don't give us much choice," Wildcat spat the words at Gaffrey.

"It's a sight more than you gave this girl," Gaffrey replied.

"I done told you," Wildcat blustered. "She ain't no white woman, she's a squaw!"

Gaffrey didn't bother responding further. He covered Jacob while his companion cut the bindings loose and carried the girl to his horse. He gently placed her in his saddle. Jacob helped her sit up. The left side of her head was badly swollen. A dried crust of blood was matted around her lips. Jacob mounted his horse behind her, allowing her to lean against him for support. He held his Winchester on the two trappers as Gaffrey mounted his horse.

"If you follow us, I'll kill you, plain and simple." He counted out the bills, stuffed them in a leather pouch, and threw the pouch at the trapper's feet. As the trio rode off into the night, Gaffrey looked back over his shoulder one last time. Wildcat Haynes drank from his jug and shouted obscenities. John Brooks simply stood there and stared at the disappearing riders. His silent stare made the hair on the back of Gaffrey's neck stand up and the knot in his gut tighten. Brooks hadn't said a word during the entire exchange, but his look said plenty. It was a look that burned deep with hatred.

Chapter 10

The moonlight filtered through the clear, cool night air onto the moving silhouettes below. Gaffrey was in the lead, with Jacob, the girl, and the packhorses, following a short distance behind. Gaffrey hoped the two drunken trappers would not be in any kind of shape to do them harm tonight. Still, just in case, he wanted to put as much distance between Wildcat Haynes and John Brooks and themselves as possible. The colder their trail the better. He looked up at the stars as they rode along in silence. There was nothing quite as spectacular as a star-filled sky on clear Montana night. It occurred to Gaffrey that the same spectacular sky filled with twinkling light that he was enjoying also sheltered the likes of Brooks and Haynes.

Jacob cradled the injured Indian girl as carefully as he could, given the uncertainty of an uneven moonlit trail. Even with his best efforts, she almost slid off his horse several times. Her periodic moans unsettled him. Wrong or right, he wished they had never set eyes on the trappers or the girl. He could tell Gaffrey was a good man—honest and decent. But this wasn't back east or down south. Things were different in the west. Yeah, Gaffrey was a definitely an honorable man--maybe too honorable for his own good.

The riders traveled for three hours picking their way over starlit trails before they stopped to make a cold camp. Gaffrey and Jacob attended to the girl first. Gently lowering her from Jacob's horse, Gaffrey laid her on an extra bedroll and covered her with two blankets. She was barely conscious. Her forehead was hot to his touch with. He hoped the fever would break by morning.

The men turned their attention to the horses. Liberty and the other horses were stripped of their gear and rubbed down with dry grass. Jacob watered them in a stream nearby and then picketed the horses on a grassy spot close to camp. With Liberty, as well as the other horses, sensitive to any unusual movement outside the camp's perimeter, the two men felt relatively safe.

After preparing their beds, Gaffrey and Jacob shared a piece of jerked meat. They ate in silence for a time before Gaffrey spoke. "I know you probably don't agree with what I did back there. After Burroughs, we don't need any more enemies."

Jacob said nothing as he chewed.

Gaffrey continued, "Maybe it was none of my business. But I couldn't let her die like that. I've seen enough of that kind of dying."

Pausing to spit out a piece of gristle, Jacob looked at Gaffrey for a long moment. "Maybe it wasn't any of your business. Maybe she's just an Indian. Maybe we should have let it go. Hell, maybe I shouldn't have even taken this job. But here I am and here you are. You did what you did. Smart or not, it was the right thing to do. Indian or not, she didn't deserve those two. Only time will tell how much it's gonna cost us."

"Yeah, you're right about that. Only time will tell. But right now, it's time to get a couple of hours of shuteye," Gaffrey replied with a yawn, allowing himself one final stretch before he pulled his blanket up around him.

Gaffrey looked at the stars and listened to the horses cropping grass. He closed his eyes. The wind moaned softly through the trees. The girl moved slightly. As sleep overtook him, the faces of Wildcat Haynes and John Brooks passed quickly through his consciousness one last time.

Gaffrey woke with the first light. He checked his boots for night crawlers before he put them on. Picking up his canteen, he eased over to where the girl lay. He pulled back the blanket to check her condition and was startled to find that she was already awake. She lay silently, looking at him in a way that made Gaffrey uneasy. He wasn't sure what it was, but past the pain, confusion, and distrust was a look that spoke of calm and strength—of a private place where she could still be herself no matter what the circumstances. He offered her the canteen, which she accepted and drank deeply from, never taking her eyes off him. When Gaffrey reached out to touch her forehead, she turned away. Then, realizing he meant no harm, she turned back to face him. With the back of his hand, he could tell the fever had broken.

Taking off his neckerchief, Gaffrey took the canteen from the girl. He wet the neckerchief and wrung it out. He began to wipe away some of the dried blood and grime from her face and neck. From force of habit, she initially stiffened at his touch, then began to relax and let him clean her up a bit. As he continued his awkward and rather clumsy attempt to wash what he could see of the girl, he heard Jacob chuckling behind him.

"How old you reckon she is?" Jacob asked.

"Couldn't really say. I reckon she's had to grow up before her time being with the likes of them," Gaffrey replied as he wiped the grime off the girl's neck.

Jacob smiled. "You sure ain't much of a nursemaid Frank. It's plain you ain't never had no girls of your own. Why don't you go fix us some breakfast and let me see if I can help her?"

Gaffrey was only too happy to oblige. He built a small breakfast fire, then checked the area closely with his field glasses. Scanning the horizon, it occurred to him that, as far as he was concerned, Montana was no longer the peaceful place it had been a few days ago. It seemed that he was accumulating new enemies on a daily basis.

As Gaffrey put a pot of coffee on the fire and began frying bacon, he marveled at the way Jacob dealt with the girl. Normally a man of few words, Jacob whispered in soft, soothing tones as he stroked her hair and offered her another drink from the canteen. With two daughters of his own, he was assuming a role with the Indian girl that he had come to know well.

Gaffrey brought them both a plate of fried bacon and bread. Jacob ate his breakfast quickly as he was accustomed to doing, but the girl held her plate close to her mouth as though protecting her food. She ate slowly and deliberately. It was obvious hunger was no stranger to her. Gaffrey poured Jacob and himself another cup of coffee. They watched the girl wipe the last morsels from her tin plate with her fingers.

Jacob tried to communicate to the girl through a combination of hand signals and Indian talk which Gaffrey could not understand. The girl communicated to Jacob that she needed some privacy. With his help she made her way to a nearby stream. Jacob left her there and returned to help Gaffrey break camp. As the two men loaded the packhorses, they discussed the girl.

"Best as I can tell she's not Kiowa, although she seems to know their language, not that I know it all that well myself," Jacob explained.

Gaffrey scratched his head. "I wish she knew English."

"Fact is, she does," Jacob said, pouring himself another cup of coffee." She speaks it right well. I don't think she ever let on to those two no-account trappers though. Probably hoped she could use it to her advantage to escape if she ever got the chance. Sounds like she learned it from some kind of missionary. Best I can tell, some kind of missionary priest spent the summer with her tribe and taught her the basics. She also has a cracked rib or two where they kicked and beat her. But other than that, it's mostly bruises. She should heal up in a couple of weeks. By the way, she says her name is Yellow Moon."

The outside will heal quickly enough, Gaffrey thought to himself, but what about the inside?

He filled his pipe with some fresh Virginia Burley he had bought at Zeke Pitts' store.

With Jacob's help, the girl mounted his horse. She was still too weak to ride behind him, so he let her sit in front, leaning against him for support. Given the girl's condition, they rode at a leisurely pace.

They finally arrived at a good place to make camp. Gaffrey stepped down from his saddle and took a deep breath. There was something about this place. Maybe it was the unspoiled beauty and the seclusion. Who knows? Whatever the reason, it was a healing balm for whatever ailed him. Here in this valley, he felt the beginning of a hope he had lost on the bloody battlefields back east. Here, he could breathe again. The world of Burroughs and the trappers seemed far away, unconnected to the beauty of this place.

Gaffrey's private thoughts were reaffirmed by Jacob's observations.

"This is mighty purty country. Purty as a picture. A man could live good off this land."

"Yeah," Gaffrey replied as he walked to the cave that would be their home until the cabin was completed.

Popping a fresh wedge of tobacco into his mouth, Jacob followed while the girl stayed behind with the horses. Liberty and the other horses enjoyed a drink from the clear mountain stream adjoining the campsite. Yellow Moon sat quietly on a rock and watched them. She later disappeared into the forest. Jacob and Gaffrey glanced in her direction.

"You reckon she'll make a run for it, Frank?"

Gaffrey drew on his pipe and exhaled a plume of smoke. "Not now. She needs to heal some. Maybe later."

Chapter 11

He watched them approach for better than two hours. The three strangers with their packhorses rode slowly into his land. He had seen their kind before. Many years ago he had watched from his silent hiding place as some of them killed his mother, skinned her, and left her body to rot in a hot July sun. His dark eyes blazed with a rage born from the pain he still carried. He had dealt with intruders before. He would deal with these new ones as well. Their kind always brought pain, whether from bow and arrow or from their thunder rods.

* * * *

The cave's entrance was partially concealed by the branches from a thick stand of Douglas firs. Both Gaffrey and Jacob stopped abruptly at the mouth of the cave.

Jacob spit and said, "What in the hell is going on here, Frank? Looks like someone don't want us to use this cave."

Gaffrey said nothing as he continued to examine five or six small uprooted firs which appeared to be a crudely arranged barricade across the entrance of the cave. It would take two men and a strong horse to accomplish such a task.

"Look at this!" Jacob shouted, pointing to what was clearly claw marks etched on rocks about twelve feet above the cave's entrance.

* * * *

The mammoth grizzly stood motionless sniffing the wind. His acute sense of smell made up for his poor eyesight. He weighed three pounds over fourteen hundred. His coat was a rich brown color and his footprints measured slightly over fifteen inches from side to side. One crashing blow from either paw could crush a horse's backbone. He was an awesome spectacle, who ruled his domain as he saw fit. His instincts for survival were ancient--as old as time itself.

The Indians called him Medicine Bear. He was both feared and respected. Three times the Kiowa had hunted the great grizzly. The lives of four warriors spoke of the massive bear's cunning and power. He was no longer hunted by the Indians. His story rather was told around countless campfires in hushed and reverent tones.

The grizzly sniffed the late morning breeze. The scent of the two men was heavy. He could also smell the horses and the Indian girl. Standing motionless at the northern end of his valley, he uttered a low, menacing growl. He could smell the beginning of their fear. His huge head swung from side to side in approval as his growl grew into a thunderous roar.

* * * *

The supplies were stored deep in the cave and deadfalls for firewood had been stacked just inside the entrance. Jacob built a small supper fire out of dried wood and prepared the evening meal. They ate heartily and polished off a pot of strong coffee. Yellow Moon's eyes followed Jacob and Gaffrey's every movement. She sat next to the fire on a blanket and ate what was offered her.

When supper was finished, Yellow Moon opened a small leather pouch she wore tied around her waist and emptied the herbs she had gathered during the afternoon into a cooking pot. She crushed them and added a small amount of water. Heating the concoction slowly over the fire, she allowed the medicine to cool before applying it to the abrasions and infected areas on her wrist and head.

Besides the thick stand of fir, a natural overhang of rock helped shelter the cave. Gaffrey and Jacob spent the better part of the afternoon clearing the entrance with the help of the packhorses. Yellow Moon was still too weak to do anything but the lightest of chores. Both men worked quickly, stopping only to drink from their canteens and eat some dried meat. Sweat streamed down their faces. Their shirts were soaked through as they kept up the pace to finish their preparations by nightfall.

"Frank, I don't have a good feeling about those claw marks. I ain't never seen a critter, even a full grown grizzly, that could make them marks. It looks like a grizzly and that ain't no good. It's like he's warning us to stay away. I wonder if he's watching us."

"I don't know," Gaffrey replied, but the tingling sensation he felt on the back of his neck suggested that he knew more than he was saying. In fact, he felt certain they were being watched. "If we can finish before nightfall, we should be safe enough in the cave."

Jacob fingered his beard. "Spect so."

The last rays of the day's light found the two men exhausted. For the most part they had completed their tasks. After finishing a hastily prepared evening meal of salt pork and fried cornmeal, Gaffrey pulled a bottle of the whiskey from one of the saddlebags. He filled his and Jacob's tin cups. "A nightcap to ward off the evening's chill."

Both men knew that it was as much for the chill of what the night might hold as it was for cool mountain air.

Yellow Moon pulled her blanket more tightly around her. The smell of whiskey made her skin crawl with the memories of Brooks and Wildcat.

While sipping the whiskey, Gaffrey assessed their situation. The girl was too weak to be of any help. The obvious size and strength of what appeared to be a mammoth grizzly was intimidating to say the least. Plus the horses, while near the cave, still had to be tethered outside where they were more vulnerable to attack.

"Jacob, I want you and the girl to stay in the cave tonight with a full fire burning. I'll sleep outside near the horses. Liberty can smell an Indian, trapper or grizzly before you or I can see him. We'll figure something else out tomorrow."

Jacob said nothing, but simply nodded in agreement. Gaffrey found a relatively safe spot against a small rock formation. He laid out his bedroll with his two Colts and shotgun close at hand.

He and Jacob made their final preparations for the night. The horses were picketed on a rich patch of grass near the cave. The fire continued to burn as the two men slept in restless snatches.

Gaffrey awoke with a start. Something had spooked the horses. Liberty was pulling against the tether line and snorting loudly. The others sounded a chorus of nervous snorts and whinnies. He reached for his guns and strained his ears for any noise. Something huge was moving through the brush, breaking through whatever was in its way. He felt the hair on his neck stand up. A light bead of sweat broke out on his forehead. Jacob appeared in the cave entrance with his rifle. And so it continued throughout the night. Moments of fitful sleep alternated with the sounds of frightened horses and weapons ready for God knows what.

The first red streaks of dawn began to appear on the horizon. Gaffrey took a deep breath and leaned back against his bedroll. As he thought about some morning coffee, his muscles began to relax. The screams of Liberty and the other horses brought him abruptly back to reality. He jumped to his feet and ran toward the horses, shotgun cocked and the Colts stuck in his waistband. The terrified horses had broken their picket line. One of the packhorses was down. The others were scattered in all directions. Where was Liberty? Gaffrey could see a gigantic form standing over his fallen horse about fifty yards away. He couldn't use the shotgun for fear of hitting Liberty. Dropping it, he jerked his colt out of his waistband and fired through the gray morning light at the roaring shape, hoping to at least turn its attention from the injured Liberty.

Grazed by a lucky shot from Gaffrey, approaching at a full run, the grizzly turned from the horse and charged. Firing the last round from his pistol, Gaffrey looked for the nearest tree. Seconds were precious. Only forty yards separated him from the enraged grizzly. His heart felt like it would explode as he gasped for breath. He raced to a medium-sized fir, lunging at a solid limb six feet above the ground. If he could just reach the next branch he could just pull himself up a little higher.

The grizzly's claws tore through his rawhide shirt and began to pull him from the tree. Standing on his hind legs, the grizzly bent the limb that Gaffrey was clinging to. The bear growled and reached up again, humanlike, making slight contact this time. Gaffrey tried to kick free with his left leg, but with one swift powerful swipe of his left paw, the grizzly fractured it below the knee. The pain was unbearable. Gaffrey fought to remain conscious as he tried to find a foothold with his right leg. He could feel his fear as the huge bear pulled him downward. His left mangled leg was caught in the vise-like grip of the grizzly's jaws. He was being dragged toward the underbrush. In a last act of desperation, Gaffrey tried to pull his hunting knife from his right boot. As if sensing what he was attempting, the grizzly shook Gaffrey violently from side to side. Gaffrey screamed in pain, as his knife dropped uselessly to the ground.

The last sounds Gaffrey heard before he lost consciousness was the strange mix of Jacob calling his name and the grizzly snorting his disgust. Jacob's voice sounded like a faraway echo of a dream while the foul blast of the grizzly's bellowing assaulted what was left of Gaffrey's senses. As blackness enveloped him, Gaffrey's last thought was of Liberty. He hoped that his old friend was still alive.

Chapter 12

Jacob had never felt so helpless. Not even the time when his wife was near death during the birth of their last child. When Gaffrey screamed, Jacob began to shout his name as if such an utterance might somehow magically make the grizzly stop his attack. Paralyzed by the suddenness and ferocity of the grizzly's assault, he watched the mammoth bear snatch a scrambling Gaffrey from the fir and toss him about like a rag doll. The girl stood behind him wide-eyed, not uttering a sound.

Jacob assumed the grizzly would finish off his helpless friend as he tried in vain to get a clear shot with his Winchester. He fired wildly in the air, hoping to divert the grizzly's attention. Then a strange thing happened. The grizzly dragged an unconscious Gaffrey to a spot within twenty yards of the cave's entrance. Shaking him one last time for effect, the huge bear dropped him in a heap and abruptly disappeared into the underbrush.

Jacob and the Yellow Moon scrambled to where Gaffrey lay and dragged what was left of him into the cave.

"Frank, you're a bloody mess," Jacob muttered as he cut the tattered remains of Gaffrey's shirt from his lacerated body. "Stay with us, Sweet Jesus, stay with us!"

Bending over Gaffrey, Yellow Moon pressed her ear to Gaffrey's mouth. "He still has breath."

Jacob and the Yellow Moon worked feverishly to clean Gaffrey's wounds and stop the bleeding. As they worked, Jacob frequently looked out, half-expecting the grizzly to return and finish what he had started.

Three hours later they had done what they could for him. Now it was out of their hands. They had sewn seventy stitches to close the wounds on his back, chest and legs. They set his broken leg the best they could and secured the fracture with a homemade splint. An herb poultice was hastily prepared by Yellow Moon. She and Jacob sat around the small fire, silent and exhausted, looking blankly at one another. Gaffrey lay next to them, unconscious. All they could do now was wait for nature to take its course.

Finally, Jacob took a long pull from the bottle of whiskey he and Gaffrey had shared the night before. After wiping his mouth with the back of his sleeve, he rose to his feet and grabbed a rifle and handed it to Yellow Moon. "You know how to use this thing?"

"Yes," was Yellow Moon's reply.

"Keep alert. I'm going to check on what's left of the horses."

Yellow Moon watched Jacob pick up his Winchester and leave the camp.

Jacob looked back at the wisp of smoke coming from the mouth of the cave one last time as he entered the forest. He wondered if he would ever see it again.

The early afternoon's light danced along the treetops and the breeze rippled through the underbrush, creating an array of strange sounds and movement. Jacob hadn't been this scared since he was eight and had to walk alone four miles to his Grandmother's house on a cold October's Halloween night. He cocked his rifle and moved deeper into the forest, stopping often to listen.

Yellow Moon made Gaffrey as comfortable as she knew how. She wiped his face with a neckerchief and added a blanket when he began to shake from the fever. She kept a fresh poultice ready as well as clean bandages. Yellow Moon was no less afraid than Jacob, but unlike him, at the center of her fear was a calmness born of patience through the suffering she had endured at the hands of Wildcat Haynes and John Brooks. As she had so many times before, she accepted her dilemma. She would do what she could. Still, Yellow Moon had to admit to herself that she was somewhat surprised when Jacob emerged from the dusk of evening with all but one of the horses in tow. Even the injured Liberty was able to follow. The arc of a five-foot laceration on his side bore testimony to the grizzly's attack.

After feeding and comforting the horses and preparing a poultice and bandage for Liberty's wound, Jacob ate some jerked meat and drank a pot of strong coffee to help him stand watch through the night. Popping a fresh plug of tobacco into his mouth, he positioned himself in a secure rock formation to the left of the cave's entrance. Inside the cave, sweat began to pour from Gaffrey as the infection took hold.

For the next ten days, Gaffrey drifted in and out of consciousness. His body was wracked by fever, then by chills as he fought to escape death once more. His groans at times sounded like a call for a small boy's mother who had long since passed away.

During it all, Jacob was amazed at Yellow Moon's attentiveness and stamina. It seemed to him as though she never slept. Applying a fresh poultice, bandages, or a cool compress kept her busy. Yet she did all this and more in a quiet, unhurried way—deliberate but dedicated. He marveled at the way she was able to calm Gaffrey when his suffering bordered on delirium. Pouring himself a cup of fresh coffee, he was amazed at her attentiveness. Swallowing the last of his coffee, Jacob was glad he and Gaffrey had rescued her. She had come in mighty handy.

Gaffrey remained unconscious most of the time, with only brief moments of clarity. He existed mostly in an in-between place—somewhere between a dream and reality. Images and experiences ran together for the most part--the smell and warmth of his mother blended with the smoke and noise of Antietam. The roar of cannon changed into the roar of the grizzly and bore down on him faster than a company of Union Calvary. But more puzzling still was the recurring image of Mary Simpson and the smell of Rosewater. Again and again her blue eyes changed color into a dark shade of brown and her calico dress became a tunic of smooth buckskin.

Chapter 13

It took the better part of a month for Gaffrey to mend well enough to ride. When they finally could travel, he found the place they were looking for within a half-day's journey. Even with his aches and pain, it felt good to finally be back in the saddle after weeks of convalescing.

Jacob turned to Gaffrey, "Do you see what I see?"

A half-smile crossed Gaffrey's face as he nodded in agreement.

The men reined in their horses at the mouth of a small cave.

"Frank, this here cave ain't all that far from our other camp. You don't reckon that old Grizzly's got any kinfolk living here, do you?"

Gaffrey forced a smile, "I don't think so Jacob. But let's check it out to make sure."

Tethering their horses to a nearby bush, they examined the cave. The entrance was only about five feet high and was barely wide enough for Jacob to enter without having to turn sideways. Gaffrey found a sizable piece of lighter wood from the base of a deadfall and lit it. Armed with their pistols, the two men made their way through the cave's entrance. Within a few feet, the height increased to about ten feet while the width enlarged to nearly five feet. They made their way slowly for the next ten yards and then suddenly the cave widened. It expanded into a huge room with a ceiling height of more than thirty feet by fifty yards wide. A small spring fed pool lay to the rear of the large room. Jacob knelt down and smelled the water, then scooped up a handful for a taste.

"This water's sweet and cold. There's enough room in here for a small settlement."

"Yeah," Gaffrey responded, "And no sign of the bear."

They spent the rest of the day exploring the cave. There were two narrow passages which ran off from the rear of the large room.

"Frank, you take the path to the right. It'll be easier on you. I'll take the one to the left."

Gaffrey agreed.

Several torches were left to burn in the main room while each of the men lit an additional torch to illuminate the unexplored passages. Yellow Moon remained next to the spring.

Jacob's passage seemed narrower and more foreboding, leaving Gaffrey, who was less mobile with his injuries, to examine the more accessible passage. Gaffrey's path was wide enough for four men to walk upright, side by side.

Gaffrey was only a few minutes into the passage when his injured leg began to throb. As if that were not bad enough, an unexpected draft blew out his torch. Pulling an extra match from his vest pocket, he prepared to relight the torch. A sharp, burning pain shot through his leg just as he moved to strike the match. He grabbed his leg and moaned, dropping the match. As the throbbing in his leg subsided, he began cursing under his breath. In the pitch-blackness of the tunnel, he flung a loose stone into the darkness. Strangely, he heard no sound. He threw another and silently counted to six before he finally heard the stone ricocheting off other rocks. A cold sweat broke out on his forehead as he frantically groped for the match. Finding it, Gaffrey relit the torch and limped forward. The passageway dropped off into a pit which was at least fifty or sixty feet deep within five steps from where he sat.

"Good Lord!" was all Gaffrey could mutter as he made his way back to the large room. "Please take care of Jacob."

Gaffrey shouted for Jacob at the mouth of the left passageway. There was no response. He and Yellow Moon waited in silence, straining their ears. It seemed like hours had passed. He was tired, his leg hurt, and he was feeling the beginning of another one of those headaches. Gaffrey closed his eyes and rubbed his temples. The cool sand and stone of the cave was beginning to feel more like a tomb than a haven.

"Frank! Frank!" Someone was shaking him. "Frank, are you all right?"

After Jacob had taken a long drink from the pool, he could hardly conceal his excitement.

"Frank, I could barely get through the opening. Then, I'll be damned if it didn't get wide enough for a team of horses to run through. I ran to the light and ended up on the other side of the mountain. It's even better'n that. There's a large ledge protected by a thick forest of spruce. I climbed up on the ledge and could see the whole countryside. There's even a natural footpath leading to the forest below. Beats anything I ever seen."

Gaffrey shook his head in amazement. "I wasn't so lucky, or maybe I was. There's a drop-off to the right. Left is the way to go. I'm just glad you're all right."

Gaffrey was in awe at nature's deception. Two passageways. The foreboding one led to freedom and the inviting one led to death, like life itself. There was no understanding nature. The best he could do was to respect its mysteries.

Yellow Moon watched and listened to Gaffrey and Jacob's conversation.

Tomorrow would be a long day.

The following morning, the men and Yellow Moon assembled their provisions and began the relocation to their new home. The horses were tethered near a thick stand of spruce at the cave's entrance while the three of them stored and arranged their supplies. Ample firewood for cook fires and lighter wood for torches were stacked carefully in the cave.

Since early morning, Gaffrey had resisted what he knew was coming. After supper he whispered to Jacob, who nodded. Building a fire in front of the cave near where the horses were tethered, Jacob fixed his bedroll just inside the entrance. Here he could be near the horses and Gaffrey, yet safe from the elements and wild animals.

In the large room, Yellow Moon made her bed near the cook fire while Gaffrey located his bedroll further away near the pool. He fingered the rawhide covered stick as he waited. The spells always took a lot out of him. He wished they would stop. Maybe someday. Each time was like being back in the war. He hated being vulnerable, as much as he disliked the pain. He would try to keep quiet. Jacob understood. He had told him about the spells after the shoot-out with Slade Burroughs and his men. He needed to trust someone and Jacob was a good man to trust. The girl was another matter. He didn't want to scare her, but she would find out soon enough about his spells. So he waited.

With the first dull thumping headache, Gaffrey lay down on his bedroll. He barely got the stick in his mouth before the rolling explosions came over him. The searing pain came in waves, like the artillery shells at Antietam. As he bit down on the rawhide covered stick, his muffled moans became the sounds of the wounded and dying. Drifting in and out of consciousness, Gaffrey lost any sense of place and time as he writhed under his blanket in pain. The sweat poured from his body and his cries of thirst were muffled as he bit harder on the stick. What shred of consciousness he still retained was filled with fear, the fear that he was vulnerable—that this time he might not make it, that the pain might take him away. And then in the midst of his suffering, a cup of cool water was offered to him and a damp rag caressed his brow. The arms of his mother enfolded him in a protective embrace as his fit ran its course. Gaffrey slept for a while, clinging to his dream for comfort and reassurance.

When he awoke, it was dark except for the embers from the cook fire and the light from a single torch. He cast his eyes toward a snoring Jacob. The remnants of his headache stayed with him, a tortured reminder of his ordeal. As he reached for his canteen, he felt her. The slight startle of their response to each other was mutual. Gaffrey could see the outline of Yellow Moon's form, reflected by the lone torch. She had been lying within a foot of him under the same blanket. He could feel her warmth and hear her breathing. Yet, he chose to say nothing.

Finally, Yellow Moon spoke, "Your suffering was great."

While Gaffrey had seen and heard her talking with Jacob, these were the first words she had ever spoken to him. Her voice was calm.

Gaffrey remained silent. He reached out and touched her hip with his hand. Touching her made him feel more secure. Gaffrey dozed off again. When he awoke the second time, his headache had diminished. His hand was still on Yellow Moon's hip. He slowly traced the outline of her form with his fingertips. Gaffrey could feel her slim waist beneath the soft, deerskin tunic, then her arm and shoulder, then the smooth skin of her neck and throat. Next, his fingertips explored the outline of her face and finally the texture of her hair. He was lost in the touch and smell of her. Like a child, Gaffrey found himself twirling a lock of Yellow Moon's hair through his fingers. He could feel her breath as he moved his body closer to hers under the heavy blanket. Yellow Moon's breath quickened as she reached for Gaffrey. She held him close for a long time, like a mother would her young.

As Jacob relit the torches and stoked the breakfast fire, Gaffrey spoke, "Thank you. I hope you don't feel I took any liberties with you?"

Calmly, without hesitation, Yellow Moon replied, "You cannot take what is freely given." Gently placing the palm of her hand against Gaffrey's face for a moment, Yellow Moon gracefully slipped out from under the blanket and began to help Jacob prepare breakfast.

Gaffrey lay there a while longer, pondering the night's experience and what it meant. He marveled at Yellow Moon's care and generosity since she had been with him and Jacob. She had nursed his wounds from the grizzly's attack and now comforted him during one of his fits. Taken from her family, abused to the point of death by the two trappers, and yet she had proven to be remarkably resilient, even tender in meeting his needs. No bitterness. No fear. Yellow Moon's actions seemed driven by something deep inside of her. When he and Jacob rescued her, he figured she would be a burden. Instead, she had turned out to be a big help. Maybe more than that.

The thought unsettled Gaffrey.

He thought of Mary Simpson. She was a handsome woman and there was no denying there had been a spark of possibility between them. Then there was his original plan to get away from people and all the problems and pain they brought with them. This valley was supposed to be his refuge. Where would it all lead to? Where should it lead to?

Gaffrey rubbed his temples with both index fingers and realized he didn't know for sure where the day would lead, much less the rest of his life.

Chapter 14

It was a cool morning in late summer, a good day for construction of the cabin to begin in earnest. The construction would be slowed by Gaffrey's limited mobility, but he and Jacob were determined to finish it before the first snow fell. They had six weeks, maybe a little longer, depending on what kind of fall season they had. Gaffrey staked out the cabin's floor plan. The main room would house the kitchen, dining area, and sitting area. Next, he measured off a bedroom to the right of the main room. He and Jacob then staked out another small room off the rear of the main area. This bedroom would adjoin and conceal the cave's entrance. The cave would insure a hidden escape route, a vast storage area for supplies, and a source of fresh water if they became trapped in the cabin as a result of an attack. The floor plan formed an L shape and was connected to the mountainside, providing a windbreak for the livestock from the bitter winter winds to come.

The foundation of the cabin would be solid rock. Gaffrey and Jacob were both perfectionists when it came to such matters. There was plenty of rock in and near the valley as well as an ample supply of clay which would be used as mortar and for chinking. Jacob hauled the most of the rock to the foundation site in a makeshift sled pulled by the packhorses. Gaffrey mixed the mortar.

Yellow Moon had a hot meal prepared when the men took a break at noon. Jacob and Gaffrey inhaled their portions of cornbread, bacon, and beans, washing their food down with hot coffee. Jacob could not help but notice the stolen glances Gaffrey and Yellow Moon directed at each other. Something was different now. He wasn't sure exactly what it was, but something had changed.

After the noon meal, the two men selected rocks suitable for the foundation and fireplace. Working with the heavy rock was hard labor. Gaffrey and Jacob paused often, drinking deeply from their canteens. Wiping his mouth with his sleeve, Gaffrey squinted at the image of Yellow Moon stacking firewood for the supper and night fires.

"She's not a bad looking woman, now that she's healed up," Jacob offered, spitting a stream of tobacco juice at a nearby weathered stump. "She's turned out to be a mighty big help."

"You could say that," Gaffrey replied, as he hefted another rock.

Jacob paused long enough to give his friend a sideways look and spitting again, thought, yeah, something has changed all right.

Yellow Moon had supper prepared when the workday ended. The two men returned wearily to the cave drawn by the fire and the pleasant aroma of cooking food.

As they savored the broiled rabbit, Jacob said, "This here is fine land, Frank. It's the kinda land a man dreams of."

"It is that, Jacob," Gaffrey replied, lighting his pipe.

Jacob sopped up the last bit of gravy from his plate with a piece of cold cornbread.

The conversation about the land and the construction of the cabin continued between silent periods of staring at the crackling fire. As if on cue, Gaffrey rose and knocked the ashes from his pipe. He went to make a final check on the horses before turning in for the night.

Jacob added several large logs to what was left of the fire and with the help of an iron poker, returned it to a full blaze. The fire burned brightly, illuminating the cool night sky. The burning logs crackled, emitting a pleasant smoky aroma. Jacob commenced to snoring. Gaffrey and Yellow Moon tried to pretend that nothing had changed.

The next week found the men laboring on the rock foundation and the fireplace. Yellow Moon kept busy preparing meals, tending to the horses, and being a lookout as the men worked. When the rock laying was finished, Gaffrey and Jacob scouted the valley for good timber. After the trees were felled, suitable limbs were trimmed from the trunks and stacked for later use as firewood. Two horses were teamed together to drag the logs to the building site. Gaffrey loved working with his hands, as did Jacob. He enjoyed the smell of fresh cut wood. The air was growing cooler and the days were getting shorter. They would have to use every available minute of daylight to finish the cabin in time.

The men fitted large timbers into walls and used clay for chinking. The rock fireplace occupied most of one end of the main room. It would be ideal for cooking and heating.

Jacob Riley was a true craftsman. He split and shaped each wood shingle that went on the roof. Gaffrey marveled at his gift. While Jacob worked on the roofing, Gaffrey split and squared the timbers into planks for wood flooring. When the roof was completed on the main room, both men went to work on the floor. The flooring was lap jointed and wooden pegs were used to secure the planks. The two small sleeping rooms were constructed in the same manner as the main room, timbers for the walls with clay as chinking, wooden shingle roofing, and hard wood floors. The doors and window framing were also made of sturdy timbers.

A large porch was built across the front of the main room to provide shade as well as shelter from the elements. Several security features were also built into the cabin. Wooden shutters were constructed for the windows which could be closed in case of attack or during severe weather. Gun ports were also cut into the shutters to give the occupants a more secure firing position. The single glass window that Jacob had carefully secured to the side of one of the packhorses on the trip back from Morristown was unwrapped. He and Gaffrey decided to install it at the front of the cabin to catch the morning sun.

On the back portion of the roof of the main room, a section concealed a hatch door which was latched from the inside. Having an angle of fire from the roofline of the cabin could also be an advantage in the event of an attack from Indians or outlaws. The thick wall timbers would be all but impervious to incoming gunfire. They built and framed heavy doors. A sturdy door was also built to the cave's entrance. Wooden planks were cut and stored in the cave for use in building furniture and other furnishings as the need arose.

After six grueling weeks, the cabin was finally completed. Moving day had arrived. As a finishing touch, a smokehouse was constructed behind and to the right of the cabin. It would need to be stocked before winter. An outhouse was also built a short walk downwind of the cabin. Gaffrey experienced a sense of genuine satisfaction as he stood on the front porch and surveyed the Montana wilderness in all its pristine beauty. He flexed his injured leg. He had been lucky it had healed as rapidly as it had. Other than walking with a slight limp and some occasional soreness in wet weather, his leg felt reasonably fit.

Several additional days were required for him and Jacob to build a small corral and barn. The fencing was completed and then water and feed troughs were built. A sturdy lean-to shelter was also constructed as an after-thought for the purpose of keeping firewood dry.

The last major chore was to stock the smokehouse. There was a bountiful supply of deer, elk, and caribou in the valley. Two weeks of hunting filled the smokehouse to capacity. Nothing was wasted. Yellow Moon carefully prepared the animal hides while Gaffrey and Jacob salted and hung meat in the smokehouse to cure.

On a crisp night in early fall, the three of them sat near the fireplace, relishing a meal of freshly roasted venison. The fire crackled and popped, filling their cabin with the pungent smell of pine and cedar. The men smoked their pipes while Yellow moon repaired a torn blanket.

Finally Gaffrey broke the silence. "We did it."

Jacob and Yellow Moon smiled. Gaffrey looked at each of them with a quiet sense of gratitude. Reaching into the saddle-bag next to his rough-hewn chair, he pulled out a rawhide pouch and handed it to Jacob. "I believe you'll find the wages we agreed upon."

Jacob nodded and placed the pouch in his vest pocket.

Gaffrey cleared his throat as he tamped the tobacco in his pipe. "Jacob, I've always seen myself as pretty much a loner, but I've been thinking lately that it might be nice to have a neighbor of sorts in the valley. If you're interested, I'd like to give you and your family a parcel of bottomland down near the river."

Jacob's eyes opened wide in amazement. He quickly looked away in order to brush aside an unexpected tear. It had taken all he could do to keep his family clothed and fed. Like any man, he had dreamed of owning his own land, but it had been a dream Jacob had never really expected to come true.

"You sure about this?" His voice cracked when he spoke.

"Yep," Gaffrey replied, relighting his briar with a burning sliver of wood from the fire.

"I'd be willing to pay for it."

Gaffrey took his pipe from his mouth and looked intently at Jacob. "Jacob, my land's not for sale and a man doesn't pay for a gift."

After several moments, Jacob regained his composure and turned back to face Gaffrey. "You shorely are a generous man, Frank Gaffrey. Never in my wildest dreams did I expect a chance like this—that I would have a chance like you're offering. I've missed my wife and children somethin' terrible. Having our own place in a valley like this, with you as our neighbor is more than I ever would've hoped for."

Breaking into a grin, Jacob exclaimed, "You've made me an offer I can't refuse! I can't wait to tell the Missus!"

A hearty handshake sealed the transaction. Gaffrey reached into his rucksack and pulled out a bottle of whiskey and two tin cups. The two friends toasted their agreement. He and Jacob drank well into the night, talking of their dreams and plans for the valley. Yellow Moon quietly finished mending the blanket and shaped a new pair of deerskin moccasins. She smiled from time to time in response to Gaffrey and Jacob's whiskey talk. How different they were from the two trappers who almost killed her. Yellow Moon shuddered as she brought her attention back to the warmth of the fire.

The following morning found the two men nursing headaches that took two strong pots of coffee to contain.

Sipping on a steaming cup of the strong brew, Gaffrey said, "Jacob, We need to make one last trip to town for supplies before winter."

"We shorley do," Jacob quickly replied. "And I want to see my wife and kids mighty bad."

After a brief discussion, it was decided that Jacob would return to Morristown for supplies and a visit with his family. He would return to the valley by the seventh day and remain for the winter. While the weather would dictate what would or could be done, the two men hoped they could complete construction of a second cabin and outbuildings for Jacob's family by late spring. While he was gone, Gaffrey and Yellow Moon would continue to finish a variety of chores around the cabin.

The men awoke early the next morning to the smells of Yellow Moon cooking breakfast. After they finished eating, she packed food for Jacob's journey while he strapped on his .44 and sheathed his freshly oiled Winchester.

Jacob saddled his horse as Gaffrey bridled one of the packhorses. They went over the supply list one last time. After mounting and saying his goodbyes, Jacob galloped off shouting a final goodbye over his shoulder. "I'll be on the lookout for ol' medicine bear. Y'all best be too."

When he had ridden out of sight, Frank looked at Yellow Moon and she at him. There was still plenty to do.

Chapter 15

Jacob Riley rode hard the first day, pausing only briefly to rest his mount and packhorse. He fingered his rifle as he traveled, half expecting trouble with every bend in the trail. Jacob ate some jerked meat as he rode and washed it down with some fresh spring water from his canteen.

He galloped into Morristown as dusk was gathering on the third day of his journey. The lights and noise of the town seemed as much a warning to him as a welcome. His yearning to see his wife, son and daughters again pushed caution aside as he pointed his horse for home. Dusk was losing itself into darkness when he hitched his horses to a tree at the edge of the back yard near the small shanty on the edge of town. Bursting through the door, his daughters, Ruth and Esther and his eight-year-old son, Elijah shouted with glee. "Poppa, you're back!"

Naomi, his wife of fifteen years, shrieked, dropping a pan of cornmeal on the floor. The entire family embraced for a long time. No words were spoken, but their sighs and tears of joy were testimony to the fierce beauty of the land they were a part of. It was a land where a delicate balance existed between leaving and returning. There had been many families who, like the Rileys, left their homes in search of a better life, never to return or be heard from again.

Naomi and the children sat in rapt awe around the fire-place as Jacob recounted what had happened to him since he left.

A chorus of oohs and aahs resounded when he told of the gunfight with Slade Burroughs and his men and rescuing Yellow Moon. Naomi brought her left hand to her mouth in horror and gripped Jacob's arm tightly as he retold the story of the grizzly's attack.

Jacob stood and gestured with his hands. "And that giant of a bear shook poor Frank somethin' fierce. Then he dropped him on the ground and looked me and Yellow Moon square in the eye. I tell you I could smell his foul breath. It was like he was sendin' us a message. 'Get off my land or die!'"

Finishing with a flourish, Jacob collapsed in his chair. His family gasped at the close call.

Jacob saved the best news for last. His voice filled with emotion as he told his family about Gaffrey's gift.

With tears in her eyes, all Naomi could manage to say was to repeat "Oh, my" over and over.

* * * *

It was the morning of the third day since Jacob had left for Morristown. An air of formality still lingered between Yellow Moon and Gaffrey. They both sensed the tension of their night in the cave together although neither one had spoken of it since. For the first two days of Riley's absence, they had maintained an unsteady balance in their relationship.

Gaffrey wiped the sweat from his brow as he leaned on his double-sided axe and observed Yellow Moon airing out blankets on the rail of the front porch. He didn't feel in control. What he felt like was the fourteen year-old boy he had been as a lad in Virginia when he was smitten by Mary Louise Stevens, a thirteen year-old schoolmate with long, blond hair. In spite of himself, he noticed every move Yellow Moon made. He swore under his breath that he would split wood until he dropped before he would let desire overtake him. And he did just that, stopping only for some cold corn bread and salted meat, and an occasional drink from a nearby mountain stream.

Gaffrey worked his axe like a man possessed, until night was upon him. In two days, he had split two weeks' worth of firewood. Taking one last drink from the stream, he slung his axe over his shoulder and started for the cabin. He walked slowly. Every muscle in his body ached. He felt confident that weariness had won out over what little, if any, desire was left. Entering the cabin, he washed up before collapsing in a heap on the bench at the rough hewn plank table he and Jacob had built.

Yellow Moon looked at Gaffrey with a sense of puzzlement as she dipped two piping hot bowls of venison stew from the iron kettle hanging by a hook over the hot coals. "You work very hard."

He nodded in agreement. "There's a lot of work to do."

She said nothing else as they ate in silence. They looked at each other as they ate, drinking cool spring water, but saying nothing. Yellow Moon dipped a spoonful of the venison from her bowl and raised it to her mouth. For no apparent reason, Gaffrey reached out and gently grasped her wrist. At first Yellow Moon tensed slightly and then relaxed. Without taking his eyes from hers, Gaffrey slowly guided her hand to his mouth. Then he took a spoonful from his bowl and fed her. She accepted the food with a calm gaze. Again, he guided her spoon into her bowl and then to his mouth. A third time even more slowly, he repeated the procedure. He could smell the desire they shared. He pulled her hand to his mouth and kissed it gently. Yellow Moon's spoon dropped to the floor.

Gaffrey kissed her hand once more and looked into her eyes intently. "I don't know where this will go--if it will go anywhere. There may be no future for us—there's a woman in Morristown."

Suddenly, Yellow Moon placed her right hand on Gaffrey's lips, silencing him in mid-sentence.

"Today is enough."

Picking up her spoon from the floor, she dipped it into her bowl and offered Gaffrey another taste of the stew. He did the same for Yellow Moon. They faced each other, chewing in silence, transfixed by each other's gaze. Slowly they moved together. Their kiss signaled an end to their restrained passion and the beginning of a spontaneous outpouring of affection that lasted well into the night.

* * * *

The morning came too soon for Jacob and Naomi. Jacob sat drinking his third cup of steaming, black coffee as he watched his wife lovingly prepare breakfast. He thought about their life together. She was a sturdy woman who possessed a big heart and smile. She had loved Jacob in good times and bad. There was no one, not even Gaffrey, who he trusted more.

Naomi handed him a letter for Gaffrey from Mary Simpson. Mary didn't know she might have some competition. Maybe she did. Maybe she didn't. Wasn't none of his business anyway, Jacob thought.

Jacob's goodbyes to his family were short and to the point. He was not a big talker, but his feelings for them and theirs for him were obvious. His children stood by their mother with tear-streaked eyes, waving to him as he rode toward town. He twisted in his saddle trying to get a last look. Naomi's wave was accompanied by an expansive, encouraging smile. Her fears remained hidden from Jacob and her three children.

Jacob's destination was the home of Elroy Foster, an old friend. He found Elroy where he usually was, working in his barn. After greetings were exchanged and several pulls from one of Elroy's special occasion jugs were shared, the two friends got down to business. Jacob purchased a wagon and enough grain from Elroy to feed the horses through the cold months. Elroy helped Jacob load the bags of grain into the wagon and then hitched his horses. After thanks and goodbyes and a last pull from Elroy's jug, Jacob popped the reins and headed toward Zeke Pitts' general store.

Main Street seemed unusually quiet for mid-morning. Bringing his newly purchased wagon and horses to a halt in front of the store, Jacob ambled inside. He pulled a list of supplies from the pocket of his new rawhide vest. The vest was a gift Naomi presented him with that morning at breakfast. He grinned when he thought about what she had said. "You wear this every day so I'll be close to you." There was nothing like the smell of fresh rawhide.

Putting on his usual ambiguous smile, Pitts greeted him. "Ain't seen you in spell, Jacob. I was beginning to wonder if you were giving your business to my competitor down in Smithville."

Laying his list on the counter, Jacob responded, "You shouldn't be surprised if I did with the prices you charge!"

Zeke nervously uttered a nasal chuckle as only he could, half way between a laugh and a moan. The list took thirty minutes to fill: kerosene, several oil lanterns, some basic fireplace hardware, including a new cook pot, two fifty gallon wooden barrels, cornmeal, beans, and a large slab of salted pork for seasoning. Jacob rounded out his purchase with coffee, tobacco, and although it wasn't on the list, two small urns of molasses as well as several personal items.

Pitts was always happiest when people were spending their hard-earned money in his store. And when Zeke Pitts was happy, you couldn't shut him up. Jacob had to admit, he enjoyed being caught up on the local town gossip—that is, until Pitts got to the latest news concerning Hart Burroughs. He couldn't help but notice that Zeke saved that bit of news for last and offered it up with no small amount of relish.

"Word has it there's a $100 bounty on the head of Frank Gaffrey, dead or alive. And I don't need to tell you, with the hard times around here, that kind of money has a lot of people interested."

Jacob glared at Pitts, which prompted him to quickly add, "Of course, I'm only telling you this so you can warn Mr. Gaffrey...you know because of you working for him and all. I wouldn't want anything to happen to either one of you." Throwing the last parcel of supplies on the wagon, Jacob pulled himself into the wagon's seat. He grasped the reins and looked down at the general store proprietor one last time.

"You best be concerned about staying alive yourself. Frank Gaffrey can pretty much take care of anything that comes his way."

That said, he cracked the reins, leaving Pitts standing in a cloud of dust as the wagon lurched forward. What Pitts didn't see was Jacob making one quick last stop at the livery stable just outside of town to purchase two jugs of homemade sipping whiskey, an afterthought given the news about Burroughs' bounty.

Jacob couldn't help but be nervous, even with the Winchester and the shotgun beside him in the seat. It was plenty clear to him that whatever happened to Gaffrey would more

than likely also happen to him. Jacob bit off a fresh chew of tobacco as he popped the reins once more, leaving Morristown
behind. Driving a wagon loaded with supplies would leave a
trail a blind drunk could follow. He drove his team hard that
morning, keeping a sharp lookout both in front and behind
him as he traveled. Jacob paused briefly to rest his horses and
check his backtrail. He ate the lunch his wife packed for him as
he rode. The wind was beginning to turn colder.

* * * *

It was as if for the first time in his life, Gaffrey had truly
lost his mind. For the next three days, he let himself go. His
desire gave way to the reckless abandon of someone half his
age. He and Yellow Moon lost themselves in each other.
Tending to the horses, gathering firewood, a walk in the for-
est--morning, noon, and night—one event after another,
seemed to fuel their passion. Sometimes intense, other times
playful, their lovemaking was spontaneous. They seemed to
lose all sense of time and place.

It had been six days since Jacob had gone to Morristown
for supplies. On the morning of the seventh day, Gaffrey returned to his senses. Placing his empty coffee cup on the table,
he looked at Yellow Moon.

"Something's wrong. Jacob should have been back by
now."

Chapter 16

Five Kiowa warriors picked up Jacob's trail the second morning out of Morristown. What had been a disappointing week, one scalp from a hapless prospector and two small mule deer, began to look more promising. Sighting the lone traveler with his wagonload of supplies brought forth the possibility of food, guns, ammunition, two horses and at least one additional scalp. The thought of it brought a ripple of enthusiasm which ran through the small band. The Kiowa were sometimes referred to as ghost warriors by the more superstitious residents of Morristown, given their uncanny ability to move throughout the countryside silent and unseen. They were known to strike and then disappear. Black Hawk, their leader, was known far and wide for his love of a good fight. His numerous battle scars and the scalps that adorned his lodge offered ample testimony to his courage and success as a War Chief.

Jacob moved along as quickly as he could as the sun arched higher in the clear morning sky. The tobacco he was chewing lost its taste as he became more certain he was being followed. His uneasiness grew despite the fact that he had not spotted anyone on his backtrail. His gut told him otherwise and he was experienced enough to know that more than likely his stalkers were Indians. Outlaws were not as patient as Indians and would have shown themselves by now. He pushed the team of horses to their limit, keeping a sharp eye on the ridgeline to his left. Jacob knew his wagon could not outrun Indian ponies. His best bet would be to find a good defensive spot where he could make a stand. If they caught him, they would kill him. Knowing that gave him a clear sense of resolve. There were no other options. As sweat poured down his face, Jacob cracked the reins and muttered to himself, "It's about living or dying."

He forced flashes of his wife and children from his consciousness as his growing fear drove him toward a place of possible safety. He spotted a rock formation several hundred yards ahead. At the same time, he could see the blur of Black Hawk break the crest of the ridge, followed by the other Kiowa. Their war cries signaled that the chase was on. A matter of seconds one way or the other would be the difference between life and death,

Jacob could hear the sounds of the Kiowa's ponies closing fast. A rifle shot seared a bloody furrow along the left side of his neck as several arrows found their mark in the wagon with a resounding thud to his left and right. Jacob fired his revolver wildly over his right shoulder as he drove the frightened team toward the rock formation. The war cries intensified as the Kiowa reached the wagon. The first warrior, a slender, hook-nosed Kiowa appeared at Jacob's left. His spear barely missed its mark. In desperation, Jacob held the reins with his left hand and grabbed the barrel of his rifle with his right hand. He swung the rifle butt into the warrior's face knocking him from his horse. Making solid contact under such circumstances was pure luck and Jacob knew it. Quickly checking his flank, he could see Black Hawk out of the corner of his eye moving to his right, tomahawk ready.

In a single motion, propelled by an adrenalin rush of fear, Jacob shouted, "To hell with the supplies," as he leaped from the wagon. He rolled twice after he hit the ground and came up running toward the rock formation twenty yards away. He was amazed to find that he still clutched his Winchester. Even the Kiowa arrow that pierced his right thigh didn't slow him down. That was when he heard the distant yet distinctive sound of a Henry rifle in the midst of the war cries.

Gaffrey's first shot missed its target and ricocheted off an outcropping of rocks. But his second shot shattered the left rib cage of Black Hawk and embedded itself in the right shoulder of his pony, sending both to the ground in a crashing, bloody heap. The remaining Kiowa quickly laid their bodies against the necks of their horses in order to present smaller targets. Gaffrey's third and fourth shots dropped two more ponies, sending one warrior flying face first into a thorny thicket. The other Kiowa ricocheted off a large boulder, breaking his collarbone. The other two warriors picked up their horseless comrades and quickly vanished over the ridge. Regaining his composure, Jacob ended the lives of the wounded Indians with his rifle.

Gaffrey's attack from long range had come as a total surprise. War was the same regardless of the ground where it was waged and who the enemy was. He had learned his lessons well in the battles down south—take the high ground, use the element of surprise and kill the leaders first. Gaffrey sheathed his rifle and took out his field glasses. He scanned the surrounding area slowly for any sign of the two remaining Kiowa. His vantage point from higher ground and the extended range of his Henry were the only reasons he had been able to save Jacob's life. Gaffrey had traded for the Henry two years back in St. Louis. He figured he might one day need the advantage of distance.

Jacob watched as Gaffrey and Yellow Moon rode into view. They found Jacob leaning against the boulder where he had taken refuge. He was covered with dirt, sweat and blood and shaking uncontrollably.

"You all right Jacob?" Gaffrey called.

Jacob sucked in a long breath and replied, "I reckon so, more or less. They weren't no grizzly, but they were close enough."

Gaffrey smiled as he leaned over and offered his friend a drink from his canteen.

He retrieved the wagon and horses. Yellow Moon applied pressure to Jacob's neck and thigh wounds. Climbing up to inspect the supplies, Gaffrey offered Jacob a snort of whiskey. He uncorked the bottle and walked over to where Jacob was resting. Taking a quick sip, he offered the jug to Jacob. Jacob drank liberally and handed the jug back to Gaffrey.

"How's the leg?" Gaffrey asked.

Without looking up from·her work, Yellow Moon responded, "The arrow is not too deep to be removed."

Gaffrey knelt beside Jacob and carefully cut away his trousers. He studied the embedded arrowhead. Jacob winced and gripped the boulder with white knuckles as Gaffrey poured some of the whiskey on the wound. He handed the jug back to Jacob as he lit a match to sterilize his knife blade. He began to dig out the arrowhead.

"You digging for gold or that arrowhead?" Jacob groaned.

Without looking up Gaffrey replied, "Arrowheads or minnie balls, what goes in needs to come out."

In less than five minutes the deed was done. The arrowhead was removed and Jacob's neck and leg were bandaged.

Jacob, rifle in hand, propped himself against the supplies in the bed of the wagon while Yellow Moon drove the weary

horses toward home. They rode in silence. There was no reason to talk. They each knew how fortunate they had been, especially Jacob. A difference of an inch or two, a few minutes
or even seconds, or a missed trail sign and the Kiowa, not
them, would be heading toward home happy and relieved. A
small tear formed in Jacob's eye, unseen by Gaffrey or Yellow
Moon, as he sipped from the jug. Now it was safe again to
think about Naomi and the children. He was alive, so his
dreams were also alive. He drank deeply as Gaffrey stopped
the horse and stood upright in his stirrups to study their back
trail with his field glasses.

Chapter 17

They arrived at the cabin as darkness was beginning to reach the higher elevations. Gaffrey unloaded the supplies and put the horses down for the night. Yellow Moon helped Jacob to his bunk. Exhausted, Jacob fell asleep while Yellow Moon and Gaffrey ate a cold supper of corn bread and molasses, serenaded by the sounds of a crackling fire and Jacob's snoring. The supplies that Jacob had risked his life for were essential to their survival through the coming winter. The lanterns and fireplace hardware, while luxuries, would add to their comfort. Drawing in the smell of the fresh tobacco, Gaffrey filled his pipe and lit it. Settling back in a rough-hewn chair covered with an elk hide that Yellow Moon had finished, he exhaled a plume of aromatic smoke. He was thankful for friendship and a warm fire. While Gaffrey smoked and watched the fire, Yellow Moon hung the best of the deer, elk, and caribou hides on the cabin walls. She then lit each of the lanterns. With the glowing lanterns and the light from the huge rock fireplace, the sturdy cabin was brightly illuminated. The night grew colder outside their mountain outpost. The thick timbers and the cabin's tight construction would help shield them against the icy winds to come.

The next morning dawned cold and gray. Gaffrey rose early to take care of the horses and other chores. Yellow Moon tended to Jacob's needs. After the previous day's challenges, today would be a day of rest. After cleaning and oiling his and Jacob's weapons, Gaffrey looked out the window. He and Yellow Moon watched the strong gusts of wind and light snow begin to fall. Winter would not be far behind. He carefully unfolded the letter from Mary Simpson that Jacob had given him.

Dear Frank,
I hope this letter finds you well.
The hotel continues to take most of my time and energy.
I hope to see you in the spring when you come for supplies.
Fondly yours,
Mary
P.S. Bessie sends her regards.

Gaffrey looked up from the letter, out into the swirling snow. Although their encounter had been a brief one, it had felt right. Mary was a strong and intelligent woman who would make any man a fine wife and partner. He had to admit that he had thought about her and their night together on more than one occasion. And then there was Yellow Moon. He didn't know for sure what she wanted. He hadn't asked her and she hadn't offered an opinion. Maybe she wanted to return to her own people. Maybe not. Taking Mary as his wife, if she was interested, made a lot of sense—Yellow Moon didn't. If something happened to him, an Indian wife married to a white man had no rights. Who knows what either woman wanted? He wasn't even sure what he wanted. What he had thought he wanted when he came to this land was to be left alone, but that hadn't turned out to be the case. Sometimes things turn out for the better, sometimes not. Gaffrey folded Mary's letter and placed it in his breast pocket as an errant snowflake splattered against the windowpane.

The fall season at this altitude was as short as it was intense. The golden leaves of the aspen and the varied shades of reds and oranges of the other hardwoods silently painted the landscape with breathtaking beauty. As colorful as it was, fall quickly retreated before the rapidly approaching winds and snow of winter. Within weeks, the temperatures plummeted to a howling twenty degrees below zero. The snow covered everything in a dense, white blanket. A thick rope, connecting the cabin to the barn and corral, maintained a lifeline between men and horses during the worst part of the blinding snowstorms. The harshness of the winter surprised both Jacob and Gaffrey as they began to experience the symptoms of cabin fever.

Yellow Moon prepared hearty meals. She was a quick study, realizing that Jacob and Gaffrey preferred more seasoning than she was accustomed to. She made each of the men a warm pair of moccasins, gloves, coats and headgear out of thick hides. Being confined to the cabin for days on end required that each of them look for new ways to entertain each other. While Jacob was a first-rate story teller in his own right, Yellow Moon could more than hold her own as she shared the stories and legends of her youth around a crackling hearth.

Her stories had been passed down from generation to generation in a rich oral tradition. She spoke of legendary warriors, relentless tribal conflict, and animals of the forest who possessed magical powers in a time when the land was unspoiled and game was plentiful.

Yellow Moon told of ancient tribes Gaffrey and Jacob had never heard of, and the sacred visions of their Shaman Chiefs.

On those cold, frosty nights he and Jacob sat spellbound like two small boys as Yellow Moon wove a timeless tapestry of life's beginning, the struggle between good and evil, and the role her people played in the epic drama. Finishing her latest installment, Yellow Moon left to retrieve more wood for the fire.

Cutting himself a fresh plug of chewing tobacco, Jacob commented to Gaffrey, "To be as quiet as she is, that girl can sure spin a colorful yarn."

Gaffrey smiled in agreement.

The snow and cold continued, unrelenting in its assault on the cabin and outbuildings. A pack horse took sick and died during a particularly cold week. After dressing the carcass, they salted the meat and hung it in the smokehouse. Gaffrey and Jacob took care of the remaining horses by rubbing them down daily and feeding them double portions of oats. Whenever there was a break in the weather, the horses were vigorously exercised.

A favorite pastime during the long days and nights that the two men took special pleasure in was to make plans for the coming spring and summer. They talked endlessly about planting and harvesting and the livestock they would purchase.

Jacob bit off a piece of venison jerky. "Frank, how many head of cattle you reckon we can handle?"

"Don't know," Gaffrey replied as he sharpened the blade of his hunting knife.

Pointing the piece of jerky at Gaffrey for emphasis, Jacob continued with his line of thought. "If we can get a big enough herd, we could graze 'em all summer in the high meadows and sell enough to help us through the winter. We could move the rest of the herd to that meadow near the cabin for the winter. Course there's wolves and cougars to think about."

Gaffrey checked the cutting edge of his knife lightly with his thumb. "And there's the winter itself."

"You're right about that. Winter can kill more cattle than the wolves and other predators."

The two friends talked well into the night. There would be a large garden, which would be planted and tended through the first frost. Wild game was plentiful and could be smoked and cured for the winter months as well. Gaffrey and Jacob both agreed that the land they had chosen to live in was a wild and unpredictable place—as wild as it was beautiful. It wasn't a land that easily submitted to the human hand. It was a land that required respect and a sense of reverence, a mix of towering forests, rock, fertile valleys, streams and rapids, and breathless views that both gave of its bounty and took extreme measures against those who didn't honor its limits. It wouldn't be easy, but both Gaffrey and Jacob were convinced that with a lot of hard work and some common sense, a good life could be found in this valley.

As the two men finished the last of their coffee and conversation, they sat in silence and enjoyed the warmth of the crackling logs that roared against the cold dark night surrounding their small cabin. Gaffrey, Jacob and Yellow Moon were each lost in their own thoughts, watching the fire and listening to a lone wolf howl its complaint to a cold night sky.

Chapter 18

December finally arrived and Jacob began talking about Christmas. Gaffrey had never been much of holiday person and Yellow Moon listened to Jacob's Christmas chatter with both amusement and puzzlement. The sub-zero temperatures continued, but the winds and snow abated. Tending to the horses, cooking, replenishing firewood, and keeping the water supply fresh were daily routines each of them shared. Yellow Moon handled the cooking with the exception of Jacob's special 'firewater' stew. His special stew turned out to be little more than several cups of whiskey added to Yellow Moon's regular recipe. Yellow Moon also did most of the mending and general cabin cleaning while Gaffrey and Jacob handled outside chores. On occasion, when a clear day showed itself that wasn't too bitterly cold, he and Jacob would also set out on a short hunting excursion. There was little to hunt during winter at this altitude other than an occasional rabbit, still the vigorous exercise always seemed to lift their spirits.

As the end of December grew closer, Jacob began to hint at the special gifts he was preparing for his two friends. At first, Gaffrey thought Jacob was kidding. When he began to realize how important Christmas was to Jacob, he tried to think of what gifts he might offer his friends. Yellow Moon kept her thoughts to herself. Her Christmas experience had been one of rape and beatings at the hands of Wildcat Haynes and John Brooks. The memory caused her to shudder.

"Yesirree. It won't be long now. You two are surely gonna be surprised!" a jolly Jacob exclaimed the day before Christmas. "Frank, me and you need to go out and find us a suitable tree. Let's take a look around after we eat."

The men waded through knee-deep snow for about a quarter of a mile before Jacob found a tree that was suitable. Although it was winter and not much of anything that breathed and moved would be stirring, Gaffrey remained cautious. His Winchester rested lightly in a rawhide sling on his right arm. The memory of the Grizzly attack was still fresh in his mind.

He and Jacob dragged the fir to the cabin where they set it up in the corner opposite the stone fire place.

"That tree sure does smell good!" exclaimed Jacob. "It's a mighty fine Christmas tree, if I do say so myself."

Yellow Moon placed a strand of colored beads at the top under Jacob's careful instruction. The two of them made strands of popcorn to wrap around the branches. Yellow Moon and Jacob found holly and mistletoe near the cabin. The green and red colors added a nice finishing touch to the tree. While Gaffrey and Jacob checked the livestock, Yellow Moon prepared an evening meal of beans and broiled rabbit. She had snared the rabbit earlier in the day while Jacob and Gaffrey were looking for a tree.

On Christmas Eve night at Jacob's insistence, he and Gaffrey shared stories of their childhood at Christmas.

Jacob gestured with his hands in describing how large the Christmas trees were during his childhood. "My Pa and Ma weren't nothin' but poor Missouri dirt farmers. But, poor as we were, they always found a way to put on a big Christmas.

There was seven of us young'uns. I was the oldest. We each had us an old sock we hung on the wall next to the fireplace. Even in the hardest times, there was always a piece or two of hard candy and a handful of raisins or chestnuts in those socks on Christmas morning. And Ma always found a way to fix something special for dinner."

Jacob looked wistfully at the fire and wondered how Naomi and the children were doing down in Morristown.

"Frank, what about you? What was Christmas like with your folks?"

Gaffrey toyed with the stem of his pipe before answering. "My father wasn't much for the holidays. I guess his father was that way before him. He worked at a bank. Christmas Eve was pretty much like most other nights. When he got home from work, we had already been put to bed."

Jacob shook his head. "That don't sound like no fit Christmas for young'uns. What about your Ma?"

Gaffrey cleared his throat. "Well, she did her best to make holidays special for me and my brother. We didn't have any other kinfolk around. She put up stockings and filled them with candy and such."

"That's more like it," Jacob exclaimed. "And I bet she fixed a special Christmas meal."

"It was special enough," Gaffrey replied. "Me and my brother always ate separate from my parents. Christmas night we usually had turkey or ham with the trimmings." Gaffrey uncorked the jug of whiskey and filled Jacob's and his cups. "Like I said, my Mother did the best she could."

Yellow Moon also spoke of her childhood memories about special winter tribal festivals. Sipping whiskey from his cup, Gaffrey enjoyed watching Yellow Moon demonstrate her favorite festival dance. He also had to admit that Jacob's child-like enthusiasm was beginning to affect him as well. He chuckled more than once in response to Jacob's childhood memories. It made him feel good to see Yellow Moon laugh at Jacob's antics. Jacob's unfinished second whiskey sat on the table. He lay stretched out on the rawhide-covered bench in front of the fire, snoring loudly. Gaffrey and Yellow Moon looked at each other. Yellow Moon laughed softly when Gaffrey smiled at her.

"You want to go outside and take a look at the moon?"

Yellow Moon laughed again and nodded.

Wrapping themselves in warm buffalo robes, they stepped into the clear, cold night. The sky was illuminated by a full moon and thousands of glittering stars. Standing close, they looked up into a Christmas Eve sky—a twinkling sea of lights surrounding a snowball of a moon. Not only did the moon brighten the night sky, its reflection off the snow and snow covered trees added to the magic of the moment. They stood quietly and observed nature's beauty. The only sound was their breathing. Gaffrey reached for Yellow Moon and embraced her as she rested her head on his chest. Gaffrey felt desire, but wasn't sure. He and Yellow Moon stayed wrapped in each other's arms for a long time before returning to the warmth of the cabin.

Chapter 19

Christmas Eve was a time of reflection and anticipation for all who believed and participated in the promise of the day that followed. For some, it was a day of great religious significance and celebration. For others, it was a chance to be with family and friends as another year came to a close. For some it was a season of gratitude and hope, while others viewed it as a time which painfully reminded them of what they did not have—of dreams gone sour and people to blame.

Gaffrey lay on his bunk listening to the staccato snorts of the sleeping Jacob above him. He thought about the events of the past year; the arduous journey from the east, finding this beautiful place, meeting Mary Simpson, and coming to know Jacob. He reflected on his relationship with Yellow Moon on the one hand, and killing Hart Burroughs' son, tangling with Haynes and Brooks, and the grizzly on the other. It had been a difficult year, but like the light of the full moon that shone through the cabin's frosty windowpane, there was hope. Even with the questions that were still to be answered, he felt a guarded sense of contentment. As he drifted off to sleep, he dreamed a pleasant image of Mary Simpson pouring him a cup of coffee. It seemed strange though that she wore a deerskin tunic.

Jacob's raucous snores belied the peacefulness of his Christmas Eve dreams. He was in church with Naomi and his children. She had never looked more beautiful in the new dress he'd bought her. The entire congregation was singing Christmas Carols. In his dream the sounds were nothing short of angelic.

Yellow Moon lay awake long after Gaffrey and Jacob were asleep. Christmas was an enigma to her. She had learned about it as a part of the story of Jesus from the itinerant priest who lived with her tribe at their summer camp many years ago. He had taught her about the birth of the Savior. The Jesus he spoke of seemed to be a man of peace, yet he was killed by his people. And his followers had killed so many of her people. It didn't make much sense to her way of thinking.

All she knew was that she felt honest affection for her two companions. They were kind like the Jesus man the Priest talked about. They were nothing like the two trappers. Yellow Moon knew she was lucky to be alive. And to be rescued by two men like Jacob and Gaffrey was more than she could have ever hoped for.

Jacob had come to treat her as though she was his daughter. Surprisingly enough, she had come to the point where she did want to please him, not out of fear, but because his approval was important to her. He reminded her in many ways of her favorite uncle, Blue Dog, a cantankerous, but playful old man who had been a loving part of her childhood days.

And then there was Gaffrey. He was a strange man, strong and courageous in times of danger, but occasionally he would get a far away look in his eye and retreat to a place deep inside himself. She knew Gaffrey was a good man who was at the same time, proper and almost timid in the ways of love. The passion they had shared confirmed his feelings for her.

Yet, he had never really invited her to be a permanent part of his bed. Perhaps, he was shy with Jacob around. Perhaps, the other woman he mentioned during the time they were alone was the reason. Although he puzzled her, she knew in her heart that she loved him. Still, it was not her choice to make. It was his. Only time would tell. If Yellow Moon had learned anything else in her difficult life, it was patience.

* * * *

In Morristown the dreams were different. The hustle and bustle of the holiday season had died down. Excited children were in their beds--most of them fast asleep. Stockings were stuffed with fruit, nuts, candy, and small toys and personal items. Exhausted, Mary Simpson's empty teacup sat on her dresser as she sat in front of her mirror combing her long auburn hair. Gaffrey was on her mind. How was he? Did he think of her? Had he read her letter? Would she see him again? She longed for him so deeply that sometimes it hurt. Did he feel the same for her?

* * * *

At a large sprawling house on a ranch a half-day's ride from Morristown, Hart Burroughs lay on his feather bed fully clothed and alone, a half empty bottle of bourbon on his night stand--his second of the evening. He could buy anything he wanted except the life of his son. Instead of dulling with time, his grief grew. As it did, so did his hatred for Gaffrey. He knew in his heart of hearts that his son wasn't a model citizen. He had spoiled him. His son was a bully who intimidated most of the town-folk. Still, Slade had been his only child, the heir to the empire that Hart had built with his own hands. Little mattered anymore to the most powerful man in Morristown—only that Frank Gaffrey would soon lay buried in the ground as cold and empty as his own heart. The thought was like a cancer inside him. Tears streamed down his face as he repeated over and over, "It won't be long Gaffrey. It won't be long."

* * * *

For Wildcat Haynes and John Brooks, Christmas Eve was like any other winter's night when they were lucky enough to get their hands on some rot-gut moonshine. It was a time to talk big, particularly about what they were going to do to Gaffrey and that no-account squaw the next time they came across them. Their holiday season was spent in a dilapidated one-room shack some thirty miles east and down-wind of Gaffrey's valley. Their only Christmas giving had been to waylay a lone traveler who had come to their door for help with his broken wagon wheel. They had given him the beating of his life before taking all his valuables and leaving him for dead.

A light snow began to fall as the temperature dropped. The full moon bathed the deserving and undeserving alike with its pristine beauty.

Christmas day didn't go any better for Wildcat and Brooks than had the entire month of December. Their shack was barely standing. The rotting floor stayed wet from snow melting where it had sifted through wide, uncaulked cracks in the uneven wall timbers. A small, rusty, pot-bellied stove stood alone in the center. The stove was mostly used for heating, but on rare occasions, one of them would sober up enough to attempt to cook something. The place they called home smelled of rotting wood, smoke soot, spoiled food and the stench of two drunks who didn't plan to bathe until spring.

Haynes and Brooks had sold their furs and mules before winter had come in order to purchase a little coffee, salt, cornmeal, salted meat and all the cheap liquor they could get their hands on. They supplemented their winter fare through general thievery whenever they saw an opportunity. With no squaw to cook for them and serve their other needs, this winter had proved to be especially difficult, and for that they blamed Frank Gaffrey. Their hatred for Gaffrey burned much hotter than their poorly tended fire.

Wildcat mumbled through sips of cheap whiskey, "We took that sorry sumbitch in, offered him food and drink, even offered him a turn with our squaw and what did that sorry sumbitch do? He stole that no-account squaw from us to keep for hisself!"

Brooks' response was always the same, "His time is coming. His account will be settled."

Early Christmas morning, Wildcat roused from his sleep and clumsily reached for an open jug of moonshine which had been set, along with two other jugs, too close to the pot-bellied stove. In a drunken half-crouch, he lost his balance and knocked over the stove, hot coals and all, onto the open jugs. Hot embers from the dislodged stove shot out like a fourth of July fireworks display. The jugs of moonshine became moving balls of fire as they rolled across the cabin floor. The wet floor emitted a sound like the hissing of snakes. Wildcat did a frenzied war dance as he tried to dodge the stove's fiery missiles and the flaming jugs.

A startled John Brooks awoke, thinking they were under attack. He began firing his revolver wildly, barely missing Wildcat's dancing backside. Both men ducked and jumped to avoid the exploding embers and the flaming jugs. It didn't take long for Brooks to realize that the flaming embers had embedded themselves in his wooly beard. The hiss and wisp of smoke rising from his beard alerted him that it was about to ignite. In his haste to get outside, he knocked the flimsy cabin door off its hinge and dislodged a support beam. Brooks dove headfirst

into a snow bank. Right behind him came his squalling partner, landing on top of him. The front part of their shack
crashed to the ground in a flaming heap.

Once he realized he was out of harm's way, an enraged
Brooks pulled his skinning knife out of his boot. Shivering in his
stocking feet, John Brooks towered over his bewildered partner.
"I ought to skin you alive. Hell, I want to skin you alive!"

It took all the self-restraint Brooks had to not kill his partner. Instead, he kicked the cowering Haynes for a full ten
minutes.

As sore as he was after the beating, Wildcat was still
grateful to be alive. He had seen Brooks kick more than one
man to death when his anger got the best of him. Ironically,
the dampness of the shack was all that kept the entire structure
from burning to the ground. It took the two trappers the better part of the day to repair the damage enough to provide
some semblance of shelter from the elements.

Both men lay on the floor with what was left of their supply of cheap liquor. The closest thing to a Christmas decora-
tion in their shack was Wildcat's red, swollen nose, compliments of John Brooks' boot.

* * * *

Christmas Day was much different in the cabin deep in
the valley. A bright, cold blue sky heralded a good day, a day
of fellowship and gratitude. Yellow Moon and Jacob prepared
a small feast. The aroma of roasting venison and broiling rabbit
filled the cabin. They washed down beans and corn bread with
spring water and strong coffee. Yellow Moon had baked small
cakes made with molasses and the last of their flour. The spirit
of the season was in the air as the three friends finished their
meal. While Yellow Moon cleaned up, Gaffrey and Jacob settled in front of the fireplace. Gaffrey loaded and lit his briar

while Jacob cut a fresh wedge of chewing tobacco. When Yellow Moon joined them, Jacob rose from his bench.

"It's time for some Christmas presents!" Jacob reached under his sleeping blanket and pulled out a section of blue calico cloth. He bowed deeply and handed it to Yellow Moon. His smile nearly lit up the room. "This here's from the same bolt I gave my wife and daughters. It ought to make you a right purty shirt and bonnet."

The usually quiet Yellow Moon was obviously moved. She retrieved two gifts from her knapsack. Each was wrapped in a soft piece of deerskin and tied with a thin rawhide string. She handed a gift to each of the men.

Jacob unwrapped his with the undisguised glee of a small child. "A fur hat with ear flaps! Just what I needed. My old hat ain't much against the cold even with that old wool scarf tying it down." Jacob tried on the hat. "It fits perfect." He grabbed Yellow Moon in a bear hug and lifted her off the floor.

Yellow Moon's gift to Gaffrey was a deerskin shirt. He ran his hand over the shirt and felt its smoothness.

"Hellfire, Frank!" Jacob exclaimed. "Try it on."

Gaffrey pulled the shirt over his head. It fit him like a glove. His smile covered his face. It was all the thanks Yellow Moon needed.

Jacob turned to Gaffrey. "I got you this pocketknife while I was getting supplies. You ain't got a good small knife."

Gaffrey fingered the freshly oiled knife. He looked at his two friends like a small boy who found his Christmas stocking full. "I don't know what to say except thanks to you both. I don't have any gifts for you. Like I said before, I'm not much of a Christmas person."

"Aw, that's all right, Frank," Jacob quickly responded. "The real fun for me's in the giving." Jacob turned to a homemade shelf next to the fireplace and tried to hide his disappointment.

Yellow Moon simply smiled and nodded in agreement.

"I'm a'going to pour us a drink of Christmas cheer," declared Jacob.

"Here, let me do that," Gaffrey interrupted. He handed Jacob's drink to him nestled in a beaded leather pouch.

"What's this?" Jacob asked.

Gaffrey had a merry twinkle in his eye. "Looks like a tobacco pouch to me."

Jacob smiled broadly. He held the pouch close to the lamp and admired his friend's handiwork. "You son-of-a-gun! You shore had me fooled."

Gaffrey lifted the flap on his pocket and groped inside. Yellow Moon's face achieved a delicate shade of red beneath her dark skin. Gaffrey slowly pulled out a necklace he'd spent several weeks working on. "This is for you."

Yellow Moon held the necklace in the firelight. It was beaded and highlighted by a bright piece of polished yellow quartz.

"I found that yellow stone near that waterfall where we killed that big buck last fall," Gaffrey commented, not knowing what else to say.

Yellow Moon handed the necklace back to him, turned her back and lifted her long, black hair. Jacob smiled. He'd suspected there was something between the two of them. Now Yellow Moon's eyes told him for certain what Gaffrey wasn't yet sure of.

Christmas came and went in the cabin in the mountain valley. For many, it had been a day of warmth and celebration. For others, it was a day that made their grief or anger all the more unbearable, lost in what might have been and determined to make sure that as far as their enemies were concerned, this Christmas would be the last.

January blew in with a vengeance. The blizzard raged. The sturdy rock fireplace stood vigil day and night. It was the coldest time the three friends had ever experienced. Keeping the fire going day and night and protecting the horses kept them busy. Jacob did his best to take their minds off the desolation outside with wild, animated stories about his adventures as a youth. The closer Jacob got to each story's climax, the harder he chewed his tobacco. Pausing, he spit tobacco juice into the fire with consummate skill and timing in order to add both mystery and suspense to his tall tales. Yellow Moon was enamored with Jacob's performances. When he was especially entertaining, she would cross her arms and throw her head back in laughter. Gaffrey had never seen her laugh so much. He liked watching her face light up.

Finally, in early April, the temperature inched higher as the sun poked over the eastern mountain range. There would still be some cold weather, but it was beginning to get warm enough for Gaffrey and Jacob to make brief forays from the cabin to hunt for fresh meat.

Standing at the edge of a thicket of lodgepole pine, Gaffrey observed Jacob feeding the horses. Yellow Moon was shaking out their sleeping blankets. Gaffrey had four rabbits strung over his shoulder as he stood on the ridge. He breathed in the cold, clear air, exhaling a frosty vapor and enjoying the peace and serenity. The unrelenting cold had made the winter difficult, but it had been one of the best winters he had been through in many a year. Yellow Moon returned inside carrying the blankets. Jacob was slowly trudging through the snow with an armload of firewood. Gaffrey watched smoke slowly spiral its way out of the rock chimney. It felt good to be alive. In spite of himself, he felt a growing sense of contentment as he thought about the beautiful valley and the cabin that was beginning to feel like a home. He rubbed the three-day stubble of beard as he savored the moment. His eyes narrowed as he looked to the sky. The coming warmth of spring would most likely bring a storm of another kind.

* * * *

The news of the bounty Hart Burroughs had placed on Gaffrey's head traveled quickly in the area around Morristown. John Brooks and Wildcat Haynes were excited by the possibility that the sweetness of their revenge might also carry a financial reward. Brooks didn't bother the dim-witted Haynes with the plans. When he and Wildcat caught up with Gaffrey and the girl, he would first get rid of Jacob before the real party began. A light bead of sweat signaled his perverse excitement as he imagined what he would do to the girl while Gaffrey was forced to watch. When he and Wildcat had finished with her, he would kill her—maybe even skin her alive before he turned his attention to Gaffrey. He planned a slow death for Gaffrey, lasting several days. He knew some old Comanche tricks that could make a man think he was dead only to be brought back for more agony. Yes, spring was coming and Gaffrey's account would be settled.

Chapter 20

Patches of green began to appear in the lower altitudes. The activity in Morristown increased, including Hart Burroughs' plan to bring his own brand of justice to Frank Gaffrey. Unlike John Brooks, his revenge wasn't driven by a perverse sense of anger, but by the grief he had borne alone throughout the winter. Burroughs kept several of his ranch-hands posted in town for any sign or news of Gaffrey or his whereabouts. Burroughs knew Gaffrey would have to return in the spring for supplies and he planned to kill him where the entire town could be a witness. When someone took an eye from Hart Burroughs his own eye would be taken as well. No more, no less.

Finishing the last of his coffee from a fine china cup, he said more to himself than to the old Chinese woman who cooked for him. "A man should get the same as he gives."

* * * *

Sheriff Gene Hill was well aware of the impending trouble. He was determined to do his best to keep the peace in Morristown and protect its citizens, most of whom were his friends. He also knew that he and his two deputies were no match for Hart Burroughs' twenty or so ranch-hands and the two hired guns he had brought in from Reno. Hill recalled finding two cattle rustlers hanging from a tree limb at South Fork Ridge six months ago. Mr. Burroughs on more than one occasion had dictated his own brand of law and justice, serving as the judge, jury and executioner. Had it not been for the townspeople pleading for him to stay on and Burroughs making sure his kangaroo courts and hangings were held out of the Sheriff's sight, he would have turned in his badge and left Morristown long ago.

* * * *

With the melting of the winter snows, spring moved into early summer. An explosion of growth and color covered Gaffrey's valley. Wild game returned. Both he and Jacob looked forward to being outside and in the woods again. Their first day out, their efforts were rewarded with a large buck. The horses, thin and gaunt from a hard winter, began putting on weight as they grazed on the tender green shoots of the valley's grasses. After two weeks of hunting and making needed cabin repairs, it was time to prepare for a supply run to Morristown. The horses were exercised daily to regain their strength and endurance. Running through the valley, they were a beautiful sight to see. A final day of preparation included trimming hooves and washing and grooming the remnants of the coats they were now shedding. Gaffrey chuckled at the way Liberty, even at his age, jumped around like an excited colt.

The blooming wild flowers provided a spectacle of color to which no artist could ever do justice. Brilliant red, purple, white, and yellow highlighted the valley which was becoming quickly covered with thick bluegrass. The melting snows and dead vegetation nourished the dormant seeds of the winter past. When warmed by the sun, they seemed to spring forth almost overnight. Gaffrey, Yellow Moon, and Jacob sat on the front porch of their cabin every evening after the chores. They would sip coffee and marvel at each day's colorful, changing landscape.

They were out of sugar and salt and down to their last pound of coffee and cornmeal. The dried beans and flour had long been used up. The trip to town couldn't be put off any longer. Yellow Moon prepared food for the journey while Gaffrey and Jacob got the wagon and horses ready for travel.

"Frank, there's a better'n even chance that all hell will bust loose when we get to town," Jacob said as he wedged his rifle behind the wagon seat.

"Could be," Gaffrey replied although he knew the odds were more likely that it would be.

"You got a plan?" Jacob continued. "Or are we just gonna ride straight into town and take our chances?"

After several moments of silence, Gaffrey responded, "Don't know for sure. I've been thinking about it."

"Well, I shore enough got me a plan," Jacob snorted.

Gaffrey stopped cinching Liberty's saddle and looked at his friend. "And what might that be?"

"My plan is to head straight to Naomi and the children," Jacob replied, grinning from ear to ear.

Gaffrey smiled.

Jacob finished hitching the other two horses to the wagon. Dried meat and corn bread were carefully wrapped by Yellow Moon for their journey and packed next to canteens filled with fresh spring water. Bandages, blankets and extra ammunition were placed next to small cooking and coffee pots.

Yellow Moon checked the cabin one last time.

Gaffrey mounted Liberty.

"You know, Jacob, I don't really want to take Yellow Moon to Morristown. Who knows what will happen? If something happens to us, there's no telling what will happen to her with her being an Indian and if the trappers are in the area. I gave her a letter to take to Mary Simpson if the worst happens. Maybe she would show her some kindness."

"I'm shore she would," huffed Jacob. "Hellfire, I ain't planning on the worst happening. I got me a wife to take care of and children to raise. But, I shore do wish you had a plan!"

Gaffrey gave Jacob a wry smile. "I'll have one before we get to town. When I know, I'll let you know."

Jacob spat a stream of tobacco juice out of the side of his mouth. "Fair enough."

He helped Yellow Moon onto the wagon seat and they were on their way.

* * * *

As he began to awake, his first impressions were the familiar odors of his home. His acute sense of smell helped him to get his bearings. His huge muscles twitched and flexed. His breathing and heart rate increased. The first overwhelming sense was that of hunger. He drooled and grunted his displeasure as he emerged from his cave, testing the wind for the scent nourishment or danger.

* * * *

As they journeyed toward Morristown, Gaffrey would periodically ride ahead of the wagon to scout the trail. He also checked their back trail from time to time. His field glasses gave him an edge as he scanned the horizon in all directions. They stopped at noon to eat and water the horses.

By pushing themselves, the three travelers arrived on the outskirts of town in the evening of the second day.

Gaffrey rode up to the wagon and pointed to a thicket of dense trees about a quarter of a mile to his left. "We'll camp there tonight. There's a good stream on its backside and it will give us good cover. We won't make a fire tonight. No sense in taking a chance on drawing attention to ourselves. Well, Jacob, are you ready to hear my plan?"

"Been ready."

"It isn't much of one, but it's the best I got. Burroughs will probably have someone watching your house. Can you ease in after midnight without being detected?"

"Does a milk-cow have teats?" Jacob replied. "Ain't no two-bit ranch hand gonna spot me. I got a root cellar don't many folks know about that's connected to the main house through a trap door. It won't be no problem."

"Good," Gaffrey said rubbing his hands together. "Tomorrow morning, I want you to have your wife go to the general store and post office. Have her let it slip that she received word that you and I plan on arriving in three days. My hope is that word will get back to Burroughs and he'll be busy planning for our arrival. While he's doing that, we shouldn't have more than a couple of cowboys to contend with when I come into town tomorrow afternoon with Yellow Moon. Your wife can get some of the supplies in the morning and we can make quick work of the rest of it. I want to get out of town by nightfall. That should give us a full day before Burroughs comes after us with any force."

Gaffrey patted Liberty's neck. "What do you think?"

"I reckon it's a purty good plan. I got one suggestion, though."

"What's that?"

Jacob nodded toward Yellow Moon, and added,"Why don't I take her with me? She'll be safer with my wife and children. Won't no one harm her while Naomi's around."

"Good idea," Gaffrey replied. "That okay with you, Yellow Moon?"

She nodded her assent. So they waited and rested, taking sips from their canteens and eating some dried meat. Gaffrey began to get the same kind of uneasy feeling he used to get before going into battle; a tingling on the back of his neck and a gnawing in his gut was accompanied by a hint of fear. It wasn't like it used to be. Now, he might have something to live for.

He had the beginning of a dream that he could lose. Even though he hated to admit it, he was also a little apprehensive about seeing Mary Simpson again. How would he feel? How would she feel? How did Yellow Moon feel?

Jacob was nervous too, but his nervousness was different than his friend's. Jacob tended to be an optimist and he was very optimistic about seeing Naomi and his children. He was a simple man, and a loyal friend. He had seen what Gaffrey could do in a fight. What Gaffrey had, a man couldn't learn. It was mostly instinct—that split-second decision that resulted in life rather than death. Jacob could see that Gaffrey was worried, but he had confidence in Gaffrey, maybe more than Gaffrey had in himself.

Yellow Moon was the most anxious of all. The last time she had seen Morristown, she'd sat battered and bruised in the back of Wildcat Haynes and John Brooks' wagon. A rope tethered her neck to the wagon seat. Her hands and feet were bound. People passed the wagon as she sat, humiliated. Out the corner of her eye, she had watched the good people of Morristown avoid eye contact and walk quickly past. She even overheard one mother tell her alarmed daughter, "Don't worry honey, she's only an Indian. She doesn't feel anything."

Although Yellow Moon said nothing to Gaffrey or Jacob, she felt sick at her stomach. She had rather die than fall into the hands of the two trappers again. To that possible end, she kept a small knife hidden in her tunic. She'd spent an hour the day before honing it to a fine sharp edge on a rock. The men weren't the only ones with plans. Someone would die before she went through another day with Haynes and Brooks. She knew going with Jacob made more sense, but no matter what the circumstances, she always felt safer with Gaffrey.

Chapter 21

J.W. was bored. For the last ten days, he and Alvin had been on constant alert for Gaffrey's return. Mr. Burroughs had been crystal clear in his orders, keep a sharp eye on Riley's home and his family and immediately inform him should they see or hear anything to do with Frank Gaffrey.

* * * *

Jacob left Yellow Moon and the wagon in a small ravine several hundred yards from his house. He slowly made his way to the root cellar, grateful for the darkness. Easing himself down into the cellar, he lit a match.

After locating the steps leading to the kitchen, he blew out the match and began pushing up the trap door. As he raised himself through the opening, he heard a familiar voice. "Whoever you are, you're gettin' ready to catch a face full of buckshot."

"Naomi, it's me," Jacob whispered.

"Jacob?"

"That's right. Your old Jacob's back."

The trap door flew back. Naomi literally pulled Jacob up by his shirt collar. There she stood in her flannel nightgown with her hair down. Their wide-eyed children peered around from behind her.

After a long embrace, Jacob explained Gaffrey's plan to his wife. Later, when he decided it was safe, Jacob returned for Yellow Moon.

It had been a good night for Jacob and Naomi. After releasing several months of pent-up affection, they lay spent in each other's arms.

Jacob kissed his wife's forehead. "It's nice to be in my own bed again."

Naomi sighed.

"I can't wait for you and the young'uns to see the valley. Gaffrey and me's gonna build us a cabin. I still can't believe he's cuttin' us out such a fine piece of bottomland. I tell you Naomi, I have to pinch myself to make shore I'm not dreamin'."

"It's about time we had some good luck. You're a good man, Jacob. You've worked hard all your life. Now you've gone and met up with another good man. All I can say is 'God Bless Mr. Gaffrey'."

"You can say that again, Momma. Me and Gaffrey's gonna shore 'nough need some blessings from above to get through the next few days."

Naomi snuggled closer. "What about the Indian girl? She seemed real nice when I fixed her a bed in the girls' room. Of course, she can stay here as long as she likes. What do you reckon is going to happen to her?"

Jacob yawned. "I can't rightly say what's in her future. There's something goin' on between her and Gaffrey. And she's been a mighty big help around the place. 'Course she may want to go back to her people. Or maybe not."

Jacob's snoring signaled Naomi that their late night conversation was over.

Naomi was up early, eager to prepare him a breakfast fit

for a king. She worried that he had lost weight and looked a little pale. After finishing a hearty breakfast of flapjacks, sorghum molasses and black coffee, Jacob patted his stomach and smiled at Naomi.

Yellow Moon sat across the table from him, picking at a flapjack. The children seemed mesmerized by her every move.

"Momma, Yellow Moon's a good cook, but ain't nobody can cook like you," bragged Jacob.

Naomi beamed with delight.

Around noon, well after Naomi had returned from the post office as Gaffrey had instructed, Jacob observed one of the ranch-hands riding out of town in a cloud of dust.

* * * *

J.W. lit his smoke and smiled to himself. Finally, they had something to report. For nothing more than the promise that he and Alvin would put in a good word to Mr. Burroughs on his behalf, Zeke Pitts had informed them that Frank Gaffrey and company would be easing into town within two or three days.

Alvin had ridden back to the ranch to inform Mr. Burroughs while J.W. had remained behind. He lounged, half asleep, on an old wooden bench in front of the Gold Nugget Saloon. He wondered if the Indian girl would be with Gaffrey. Talk had it that he had stolen her from two trappers.

* * * *

Jacob went to the front room. He pulled aside the white linen curtains and checked once again on Burrough's remaining lookout. J.W. was back at his post, rolling a cigarette and looking bored.

Jacob chuckled. "So far, so good."

About mid-afternoon, Jacob sent his son, Elijah, to fetch his friend Elroy Foster. Gaffrey's plan was a good one, but even good plans sometimes needed some fine-tuning. Over cups of hot, black coffee, Jacob and Elroy discussed the best way to take care of the lookout at the Gold Nugget. Given J.W.'s frequent visits inside, Jacob reckoned the cowboy wouldn't be too alert. Elroy agreed with his assessment. Checking his pocket watch, he figured Gaffrey would be rolling into town within the hour.

After watching J.W. enter the saloon for some more refreshment, Jacob kissed Naomi and held her an extra few seconds. He tossed Yellow Moon a reassuring look and slipped out the back door. A narrow alley between the Gold Nugget and Zeke Pitts' general store led to an old storage shack. After giving Elroy a signal, Jacob positioned himself behind the saloon, hidden from sight.

Elroy rushed up to J.W. as if out of breath. "Mister, don't you work for Hart Burroughs?"

"What if I do? What's it to you?" replied the ranch hand, feeling a sense of confidence and mellowness that only cheap whiskey can bring.

"Well, ain't there some kind reward for information regarding the whereabouts of a Mr. Frank Gaffrey?"

"There might be," J.W. cleared his throat and spit. "Anyways, I already know when Gaffrey will be arriving. We'll be more than ready for him. Why don't you run along on home old man before you hurt yourself?"

Elroy stood where he was, unfazed by the cowboy's rudeness. "Then, you must know Gaffrey's already here--that he and the Indian girl circled around and eased in the backside of town on the old north trail."

J.W. jumped to his feet and grabbed Elroy by the collar. "Where is he?"

Elroy sputtered, "But what about my reward?"

"You'll get your reward in due time. Right now you better tell me where the hell he is," J.W. shouted.

"Well all right," Elroy continued. "I saw him ease through the back door of the livery stable. He left the Indian girl in the shed behind the Gold Nugget."

Releasing his grip on the old man, J.W. assessed the situation. There was no way he was going to tangle with Gaffrey one on one, but the girl was a different matter. He could easily overpower her and return with her to the ranch which might provide Mr. Burroughs some insurance where Gaffrey was concerned. It might also mean a little something extra for him on payday. On the other hand, if he let Gaffrey and company re-supply and slip out of town—JW didn't even want to think about that.

Shoving Elroy out of the way, he said over his shoulder as he walked down the alley, "Like I said old man, git on home before you get hurt."

JW didn't even take the leather thong off his revolver as he hurried toward the shed. It wouldn't take much to subdue an Indian girl. He rounded the corner of the Gold Nugget. All he saw was the blur of a sturdy oak axe handle as it caught him squarely between the eyes with all the gusto Jacob's two-handed grip could muster. Elroy and Jacob dragged the unconscious ranch hand into the shed and bound and gagged him.

"Well, what do you think, old man?" a smiling Jacob asked his friend as they walked the back way toward Jacob's house.

"I think if you hadn't taken care of that worthless excuse of a cowboy, I would have had to whip his ass myself," Elroy, who weighed all of 130 pounds soaking wet, replied.

Chapter 22

Gaffrey arrived with the wagon within the hour. When he heard how Jacob and Elroy Foster had taken care of Burroughs' lone watchman, he slapped the two men on the back in approval. "Gentlemen I think we might have time for a quick drink before we visit Mr. Pitts' store."

Elroy and Jacob ordered a beer while Gaffrey, as was his custom, ordered a shot of whiskey and a cup of hot coffee.

Betty commented as she poured the coffee, "It sure is good to see you again Mr. Gaffrey."

"It's good to see you, Betty."

"Ain't too many cowboys drink coffee with their whiskey. I saw you do the same last time you was here. That's most peculiar, wouldn't you say Mr. Gaffrey?"

Gaffrey finished his whiskey and took a long sip of his coffee before he answered. He noticed that Jacob and Elroy were awaiting his response with amusement.

"Betty, it's nice to see you haven't lost your gift of gab since I last saw you. By the way, your coffee's as weak as your whiskey," Gaffrey commented with a smile as he laid four bits down on the bar. "This is for me and my friends."

Betty laughed good-naturedly as the three men departed and called after them, "You all don't be a stranger!"

With the immediate pressure from Burroughs off, the first order of business was to take care of the horses.

Gaffrey hadn't told Jacob and Elroy that while they were celebrating, he had kept an eye on the two men at the left corner table. They didn't fit with the other saloon patrons. They were a little too quiet and had positioned themselves to cover any angle of the room with a good field of fire. They were dressed like ranch hands, but their hands weren't calloused and their faces weren't weatherworn. They hadn't been spending much time outside in the elements. He couldn't help but wonder if they were hired guns paid for by Hart Burroughs. Maybe they were. Maybe not.

Gaffrey knew if he, Jacob and Yellow Moon could leave by tomorrow afternoon, they had a good chance to avoid an outright confrontation with Hart Burroughs. Wildcat Haynes and John Brooks were another matter. He had no way to know where they were.

Gaffrey and Jacob groomed and fed the horses. They selected and paid for two healthy mules that could be used for hauling supplies and plowing. The mules could also be ridden if one of the horses went down. They were hardy and durable animals, useful for a number of different purposes.

After completing their purchase, Jacob announced, smacking his lips, "Boys, it's time for supper! I know that Naomi has outdone herself. You ain't never ate food like you're about to partake of."

Gaffrey, Elroy and Jacob headed toward Jacob's house across from the Gold Nugget. Gaffrey kept a sharp eye out as they passed the saloon. The closer they got to Jacob's home, the more he could smell the intoxicating aroma of home cooking. It was enough to make a man's stomach growl.

Naomi fussed over the table as they sat down to eat, rearranging platters of food and worrying about things getting cold. Finally, Jacob said grace and the meal began in earnest. Heaping platters of fried chicken and smoked ham were passed around, followed by mashed potatoes and gravy and green beans that had been put up last fall. Large, cathead biscuits with real butter and molasses on the side were offered hot from the oven as soon as a plate was spotted without one. The feast was washed down with fresh milk, cold from the springhouse, and strong, black coffee.

Just when they thought it was over, Naomi and her two daughters came forth from the kitchen as though they were marching in a parade. Each one carried a different homemade pie. Naomi came first, hoisting a steaming apple pie in front of her for all to admire. She had taken great care in baking it because apple pie was Jacob's favorite. She was followed in quick succession by Ruth and Esther with cherry and rhubarb pies. The pies were eaten slowly, followed by more coffee.

"Thank you, Naomi, and you girls as well, for such a fine meal," Gaffrey said as he pushed himself from the table.

"Yes, thank you," echoed Yellow Moon.

Elroy Foster mumbled his appreciation as well.

Jacob, beaming with pride, stretched back in his chair. "Can't nobody cook like my Naomi!"

"Oh hush," Naomi responded with a half-hearted reprimand and a wide smile on her face.

After the table had been cleared, Jacob produced an old fiddle. His son, Elijah, pulled a harmonica from his worn, overall pocket.

"It's time for some entertainment," Jacob announced.

While Jacob couldn't carry a tune if his life depended upon it, he could sure play a fiddle. His son was even better on the harmonica. While the two of them played with gusto, Naomi and the two daughters danced and sang. Elroy joined in when he could remember the words. The celebration went on for several hours. Even Gaffrey caught himself humming along on several tunes. He noticed Yellow Moon smiling in her quiet way and tapping her foot to the music from time to time. Everyone did, indeed, have a good time.

Gaffrey thought back to his own childhood memories of family and celebrations. There had been some good times before things went bad, before he even quit thinking about the difference between good and bad. The war had surely changed him. He had gone from a man full of dreams to a survivor chased by nightmares—someone who no longer cared that much if he survived. It was that attitude that had given him an edge, had made him dangerous to those who might wish to harm him.

Sipping his coffee and listening to the music, he knew he still had the edge, but he wasn't sure it was as sharp. He was beginning to realize that a dream or two might still be in him. Such knowledge made him a little more than uneasy. Saying goodnight to his friends, Gaffrey knew he would need all the edge he could muster for what lay ahead.

Chapter 23

Naomi had breakfast ready at sunrise. After last night's meal and the tension that the day promised, Gaffrey settled for several cups of black coffee. When Jacob had finished eating, the two of them went over the supply list one last time. After loading Jacob's plow and some tools on the wagon, they retrieved the horses and mules from the livery stable. They hitched the horses to the wagon and tethered the mules to its rear gate. It was time for family goodbyes—goodbyes filled with hope for a new future and tension for what lay ahead.

Gaffrey and Yellow Moon thanked Naomi and the children. Naomi handed them several carefully wrapped parcels of leftovers, enough to last several days.

Naomi was a perfect example of hospitality. In many ways, she was much like her husband, strong, generous and to the point. When it came Jacob's turn there were plenty of tears, kisses and hugs. This parting was easier than the last one had been. Before, there was only uncertainty and even desperation. Now, Gaffrey was a friend. He and Yellow Moon were like family. And with some luck, a new and better life awaited the Rileys.

Gaffrey had risen before the others. He'd surreptitiously

checked out the town to determine the whereabouts of the two men he had noticed at the Gold Nugget the night before. There was no sign of them. The ranch hand who rode to Hart Burroughs' ranch would not have had time to return in force with Burroughs and his men. J.W. was awake, but still gagged and trussed up like a Thanksgiving turkey. He also checked out possible places of ambush, quick exits and hiding places. He paid particular attention to Zeke Pitts' store since that would be their last stop before leaving for the valley. If there was to be trouble, Pitts' place or the edge of town were the most likely places it would occur. By his calculations, it would be early afternoon before Burroughs and his men arrived in Morristown. God willing, he, Jacob and Yellow Moon would be long gone by then.

Walking down a back alley in the first gray rays of the new day's light, Gaffrey thought about Mary Simpson. He knew he should see her, he owed her that much. On more than one occasion he'd thought of their night together, but not as often as he used to. He excused himself saying he'd face Mary after the Burroughs situation was resolved. But he knew such reasoning was only partially true. It was also true that while he could be courageous under fire, he was also something of a coward when facing difficult situations with women. Gaffrey wasn't sure what to do about Yellow Moon and Mary Simpson, so he simply did nothing. That is why he was surprised when a voice greeted him through the early morning mist.

"Hello Frank."

Startled, he peered into the shadows. It was none other than Mary Simpson. Gaffrey felt awkward, like a guilty schoolboy, for not making an effort to see Mary. Even in the early morning light, he felt his face turning red.

"Weren't you even going to come by and say hello?"

Looking down at the ground, Gaffrey mumbled, "I wanted to Mary, but time's short this trip. With the Hart Burroughs trouble and all." Looking into her face, once again he felt the pull of whatever had drawn him to her so many months before. "I did want to see you. I guess I just didn't know what to say."

"You don't have to say anything." She reached up and touched his cheek with her fingertips. "You'll come to see me when you're ready. Just don't wait too long." That said, Mary turned and quickly disappeared back into the shadows.

Frank stood for a few moments. He was drawn to Mary's touch. And then there was Yellow Moon. But, now wasn't the time. First came Burroughs, then the rest of his life.

After a final goodbye to Naomi and the children, Gaffrey mounted Liberty. Jacob helped Yellow Moon into the wagon and climbed up after her.

Jacob slapped the reins across the horses' backs. "Let's get this show on the road."

Gaffrey said nothing as he followed the wagon, watching for any sign of trouble.

Jacob had learned long ago to trust his friend's instincts and that when the time came, Gaffrey would tell him what he needed to do. When two friends trusted each other the way Jacob and Gaffrey did, words weren't so important. A look or glance, a subtle gesture that was only detected by one or the other was all that was needed.

Jacob and Yellow Moon entered Pitts' store ahead of Gaffrey. He lingered in a corner behind a large stack of burlap bags of feed and near the window.

"Well, hello Mr. Riley and Mr. Gaffrey! It's good to see that you're safe and secure," Zeke Pitts whined. "Who's your friend?"

As if on cue, Pitts' slumbering, spotted hound whined in his sleep.

Jacob thrust the supply list toward Pitts. "Just fill the list."

"Indeed, I will do just that," replied the simpering storeowner. He pursed his hands together, anticipating a sale similar to Gaffrey's last one.

As Pitts stacked boxes of ammunition, sacks of flour, cornmeal and beans on the counter, he looked at Gaffrey standing near the window and intoned, "Can I get you something Mr. Gaffrey?"

Gaffrey said nothing but looked at Pitts in way that made the storeowner break out in a sweat.

He turned his attention back to the supply list and whispered to Jacob once again in a lower hushed tone, "Mr. Riley, I was worried about you and Mr. Gaffrey. You know, with the reward and all. One hundred dollars, dead or alive, would tempt a lot of men."

Spitting tobacco juice on Zeke Pitts' counter to make a point, Jacob's eyes narrowed as he spoke, "That temptation include you, Pitts?"

"Of course not! How could you think such a thing?" Pitts quickly replied, feigning all the self-righteous indignation he could muster.

"Just remember," Jacob added, "'dead or alive' can also go for anyone who tries to collect that reward money." To emphasize his point, Jacob placed his revolver on the counter in front of him. That gesture alone seemed to light a fire under

Pitts as he scurried to and fro with all the haste his skinny frame could afford him in filling the order.

From out of nowhere came another familiar voice. "Howdy little squaw woman, how about helping out two old friends?"

John Brooks stepped through the front door. He smiled and snarled at the same time, showing what was left of his yellow, crooked teeth, "Did you miss us?"

Wildcat Haynes reeked of cheap liquor. He stood behind Brooks grinning from ear to ear.

Jacob reached for his revolver.

"I wouldn't do that if I was you," Brooks offered as he leveled his rifle at Jacob's mid-section.

Dropping his hand back to his side, Jacob glanced sideways at Yellow Moon. Although she seemed composed, he could see she was shaking. Her trembling added considerably to Brooks and Haynes' enjoyment.

Wildcat could keep quiet no longer. "There ain't no need for you to take a chill and shake little girl. Yore new owners must not of taken good care of you. Don't you worry, me and ol' Brooks will soon warm you up right proper!"

The two trappers both guffawed. Unnoticed, Pitts' hound roused from his slumber. A long forgotten voice caused his ears to perk up. His owner tried to intervene.

"Please gentlemen. Take your differences outside. I have..."

Wildcat interrupted Pitts in mid-sentence. "Shut up yer whining Pitts. We ain't no gentlemen no more'n you are. Besides, we ain't got started with the fun yet. Ain't that right, John?"

Brooks had tired of the banter and spoke directly to Zeke

Pitts, "Where's Gaffrey?"

Pitts would have certainly answered him given the chance, but the old hound had heard enough. Wildcat's second comment touched a nerve deep in the old dog's psyche. It triggered memories of the day in the alleyway when he'd attacked a drunken Haynes. He felt like the cougar that a delirious Haynes imagined him to be.

That incident had occurred several years ago, but Reginald, as the dog was known by the townspeople, hadn't forgotten. He only had two or three good teeth left. His life now consisted mostly of begging for food, an occasional snarl that ended up sounding more like a whimper, and frequent swift kicks by Zeke Pitts' customers.

The old hound had Wildcat Haynes' number and wasn't about to miss his chance now. For all his cowering and the kicks he had endured, he was going to make Wildcat Haynes pay. The hound sprang into action, sinking his three good teeth into Wildcat's left calf. He tore the buckskin britches with a fury, shaking his head wildly from side to side. Haynes fell backwards, screaming, turning over a wooden barrel half full of overripe apples.

Brooks reacted to the old hound's attack with a startled yelp.

The unexpected distraction allowed Gaffrey to quickly step from the shadows and smash the barrel of his shotgun into Brook's face. The force broke Brooks' nose and drove him back against the counter. Thinking of the reward, Pitts reached under the counter for his revolver, but Jacob jerked him up like a sack of corn meal. His feet flew over the counter and he landed on the wood floor with a heavy thud. Pleading for release was to no avail. Jacob had long been sick of Pitts' self-righteous greediness. He expressed his frustration by grasping the squalling storeowner by his collar with one hand and the seat of his pants with other. He threw him head first through his finely lettered plate glass window out into the street.

A bloodied Brooks pulled a hunting knife from his boot and raised it to strike. Before Jacob could move to act, Gaffrey stumbled backwards against the overturned barrel. He knocked over a display, sending canned goods rolling in all directions as he fell.

Suddenly, a small hand appeared from behind Brooks. The steel blade of a knife flashed. In one movement, the knife became embedded between the trapper's legs. Blood puddled on the floor between his legs before the blade was withdrawn. Brooks screamed in agony and grabbed his bleeding crotch as he doubled over headfirst onto the floor.

Holding his hunting knife with one hand and his injured groin with the other, he flew to his feet. His face was contorted in anger and pain. He reached for Yellow Moon. Gaffrey scrambled to his feet and slammed the butt of his shotgun in the small of Brooks' back. Brooks recoiled in pain as he fell against the counter top. Jacob followed full-force with the broad side of a shovel blade to the side of his head. John Brooks crumpled to the floor, unconscious.

Gaffrey quickly surveyed the carnage. Brooks lay in a bloody heap. Gaffrey picked up the trapper's hunting knife and dropped it in a barrel of pickles. Pitts sat on the wooden walkway, crying and picking glass slivers from his bloodied, baldhead. Haynes was nowhere in sight, but Gaffrey could hear him hollering and the old hound barking in response. Confident no immediate threat remained, Gaffrey turned his attention to Yellow Moon.

"Are you all right?"

Although Yellow Moon nodded in the affirmative, Gaffrey could see that she was still trembling. He gently took the bloodied knife from her hand and embraced her.

Jacob looked out the window at the gathering crowd. "That was one hell of a close call."

Stroking Yellow Moon's hair, Gaffrey agreed with his friend. "Yeah, we were lucky. Now, we better get a move on. We need to get as much of a head start on Burroughs as possible."

Regaining her composure, Yellow Moon picked up a five-pound sack of flour. "Let's go."

Jacob threw a burlap bag of horse feed over each shoulder. "You heard the lady."

Gaffrey grabbed the boxes of ammunition and headed for the wagon.

A small group of townspeople gathered in front of Pitts' store to observe the ruckus. Pitts sat outside, dazed. He was more worried about the cost of replacing his window and the fancy lettering than his own injuries. Brooks lay inside, battered, bleeding, and unconscious.

Several of the men who had watched the melee, roared with laughter at the sight of Wildcat Haynes stumbling down main-street. Wildcat cursed for all he was worth as he high-stepped and swatted at the old hound that pursued him. He hollered every time the hound's three good teeth found their mark.

"Lordy, Lordy, somebody help an old man. Somebody shoot this devil!" Wildcat's voice could be heard from one end of the street to the other.

The money for the supplies sat folded neatly under a can of peaches on the counter top next to the tobacco stain where Riley had spit.

Jacob cracked the reins and the heavily loaded wagon lurched forward. He and Yellow Moon led the way. Gaffrey followed on Liberty.

Mary Simpson watched quietly from behind her curtain across the street.

Chapter 24

They didn't stop for a mile or two, even though Gaffrey knew they needed to regroup. He rode cautiously, keeping a close eye on the surrounding countryside. He finally spotted a rock outcropping that looked like a good place to rest. He motioned for Jacob to pull the wagon into a dense stand of hemlocks.

Jacob cut a fresh wedge of chewing tobacco and popped it into his mouth. "Why we stopping, Frank? We got a long ways to go before nightfall."

Gaffrey took his canteen from the horse's saddle and took a long drink. He wiped his mouth with his shirtsleeve. "We need to get our bearings before we go any further. Something's not right."

"What do you mean? Looks to me like things are well in hand as long as we don't lollygag around here too long and give Burroughs a chance to catch up with us."

Gaffrey chewed on a toothpick, deep in thought while Jacob fretted and Yellow Moon sat with her hands folded.

"Naomi is a good woman. And your children are kind," Yellow Moon said to Jacob.

"She is a good woman. And a fine wife and mother," he replied.

"It is good that you have such a family."

"Truer words have never been spoken. Naomi and the young'uns took a shine to you. The girls said they've never seen hair as pretty as yours."

Gaffrey interrupted Jacob and Yellow Moon's conversation. "I think it's best if you and Yellow Moon follow the old south fork road and circle around White River Falls before rejoining the trail we originally took to Morristown."

"You sure about that Frank?" Jacob asked. "That route may take us a full day or a day and a half longer."

Gaffrey looked intently at Jacob and Yellow Moon. "I'm not sure of anything. I just think it's the best way to return to the valley."

Jacob had seen that look before and since he trusted his friend completely, he grunted in agreement.

Turning Liberty toward the original trail, Gaffrey added, "I'm going to look around. I'll meet up with you two later."

Popping the reins, the wagon creaked forward toward old south fork road. Jacob shouted, "We'll wait for you at the falls."

Maybe he was wrong, maybe he was right. All he had was his instinct—the hair standing up on his neck and the knot in his gut telling him things didn't fit. He didn't know why but he was going to try to find out. Liberty broke into a leisurely gallop as Gaffrey kept a sharp eye on the horizon.

The buckboard popped and groaned along the rocky trail. "This here's gonna be one rough ride," Jacob said to no one in particular. "I know Frank's got his reasons, but I sure wish I knew what the hell they were."

Yellow Moon reached across and patted Jacob's shoulder reassuringly.

Gaffrey had been riding for a little over an hour when he stopped. After ground hitching Liberty, he snaked his way up toward the top of the ridge and whispered, "I'm about to find out if my hunch was right."

Gaffrey worked his way up the slope. Since there was little useful groundcover, he crouched and crawled between rocks and bounders. He slithered on his belly the last few yards, the rocky ground digging into his elbows. Gaffrey pulled out his field glasses from the small knapsack he had strapped onto his back. As he adjusted the focus, a booming voice from the other side of the ridge sent a chill up his spine.

Mr. Burroughs, you do have a flair for the dramatic. You are a man of history. You want your revenge at the right time and the right place. I'm just glad I won't be able to oblige you.

There, at the exact spot in the small canyon where his son had been killed, Hart Burroughs was ranting and waiting with a half dozen of his ranch hands and the two gunmen Gaffrey had spotted in Morristown from the saloon. Although they were well hidden from the trail below, their location was easily observed from Gaffrey's higher vantage point with the help of his field glasses. He also quickly identified two lookouts hiding behind a rock formation a quarter of a mile below the ambush sight.

Yessir, Mr. Hart Burroughs is looking for some poetic justice, but it won't come today—maybe someday—but not today, Gaffrey thought as he made his way down the slope.

White River Falls were beautiful in a modest way. White River was more like a large, meandering stream than a true river. The falls weren't very high, but rather a series of several smaller falls with three and four foot drops. Of course, when the spring rains came, the river would become a raging torrent, swelling to five or six times it's normal size.

Jacob and Yellow Moon sat around a campfire made of deadfalls. The warmth of the fire warded off the cool night air.

Jacob sipped hot coffee and poked the fire with a stick while he mused to Yellow Moon about the day's events and Gaffrey's whereabouts.

"Your knife came in right handy back at Pitts' store. You was as bold as a sore-tailed mountain lion."

Yellow Moon didn't respond but her expression was clear. She was still frightened and would do the same again without hesitation.

Reaching for the coffee pot to pour himself another cup, he was startled to hear a voice within several feet of his right shoulder say, "How about pouring me a cup while you're at it?"

The unexpected appearance of Gaffrey squatting so close to him almost caused Jacob to fall into the fire. Yellow Moon had no reaction except for a quiet smile. She had heard Gaffrey long before she saw him.

"Good Lord, Frank, you 'bout scared me to death!"

Gaffrey chuckled softly as Jacob poured coffee into his outstretched cup.

"It ain't all that funny Frank. One of us could 'a got hurt."

Gaffrey revealed to Jacob and Yellow Moon what he had observed that afternoon. After he finished, the three of them sat in silence.

Jacob emptied the rest of his coffee in the fire. "I ain't never seen a man who's got the instincts you do. We are all mighty lucky, mighty lucky."

Gaffrey scratched his chin. "Sometimes instincts aren't enough. All we've done is buy some time. For better or worse, nothing is ever really over. Maybe all we ever do is buy as much time as we can, until our time runs out."

With a puzzled expression, Jacob added, "Frank, I don't know if I follow what you're getting at, but I'm sure glad we're riding together."

Yellow Moon held Gaffrey in her gaze through the shadows of the firelight. She knew exactly what he meant. There was only so much time you could buy, but you could make the time you have mean something good if you had a purpose.

The hoot owl sang its lonely ballad and the fire crackled as they drifted into a light sleep.

Chapter 25

While Gaffrey, Jacob, and Yellow Moon slept, serenaded by the distant, murmuring sounds of White Water Falls, Hart Burroughs stood on the very spot where Gaffrey had killed his son. He cursed both his bad luck and misfortune while his men and the hired guns sat on their horses in silence. Burroughs paced back and forth around a roaring fire. He vented his rage and kicked at a dead tree stump for emphasis.

"That no-account murdering son-of-a-bitch who killed my boy will get what he gave. Anybody, I mean anybody, man or woman, who gets in the way will pay the same price!" Stabbing an accusing finger at the two hired guns, he turned his attention to them. "What in the hell am I paying you two for besides drinking whiskey and leading me on a wild goose chase? If you can't find Gaffrey, I'll find someone who can. Do I make myself clear?"

Both men dropped their heads.

Burroughs bellowed, "Where's my horse?"

His foreman, Powder Falen, quickly brought his mount forward. Slamming himself into the hand-tooled saddle, Hart Burroughs pulled a silver flask from his coat pocket and drank from it long and hard.

"How do we get to Gaffrey's cabin?" he asked Falen.

Powder hesitated before answering. "No one really knows. I sent out a couple of men when spring broke, but they weren't able to pick up the trail."

Burroughs took another long drink. He hurled the empty whiskey flask into the darkness in disgust. His voice was quieter now and more determined. "I know who can find them. At first light, go find Brooks and his worthless sidekick and bring them to the ranch. Let them know what I want and that they will be well paid for their services. While you're rounding the two of them up, the rest of us will return to the ranch and get ready. We'll head out at sunrise day after tomorrow. You got all that?"

"Yessir," his foreman quickly responded, glad Burroughs' attention was off him for the moment.

Soft-spoken by nature, Powder had earned the nickname in part because of his expertise with gunpowder. Four years ago, he'd been dynamiting stumps while clearing land for Hart Burroughs. A quick fuse had resulted in an explosion that had left him injured and unconscious for several days. Doc Powell wasn't even sure for a time if Falen would live. At first, Powder could talk little, but eventually fully regained his speech. Naturally quiet, he became a man of fewer words still. After the explosion, his hair turned white. Burroughs began calling him 'Powder' and everyone else followed suit. Although he lost most of the hearing in his left ear, he compensated for his loss by keen observation and attentiveness to whatever happened to be going on around him.

With clear, blue eyes and neatly trimmed white hair, Powder's quiet, deliberate gaze elicited respect from whomever he was around. When he spoke Burroughs' orders, the hands listened and responded without question.

* * * *

Hart Burroughs cinched his wool coat more tightly around him. It was colder than usual for an early summer. Two supply wagons and a chuck wagon were loaded to the hilt. One carried nothing but ammunition, extra rifles and a box of dynamite. Powder would take care of the explosives. The second wagon carried provisions including tents to house twenty men. The chuck wagon carried cooking gear and some first aid supplies.

Burroughs surveyed his small army. They were good men, for the most part, and he didn't take lightly putting them in harm's way. He also agreed with his foreman that John Brooks was as mean as a snake and not to be trusted. But whether he liked it or not, he was convinced Brooks was the man to lead him to Gaffrey. He was willing to make a deal with the devil himself to get his hands on the man who had killed his only son. His thoughts were interrupted by the smell of cheap whiskey and the voice of Brooks.

"We shorely do thank you for the use of these two horses."

"Just lead me to Gaffrey."

"Consider it done," a grinning Brooks replied.

Burroughs spurred his horse and rode toward the lead wagon. He muttered to himself, "When you make a deal with the devil sometimes you get more than you bargained for. So be it."

Wildcat Haynes, who had almost no vision in his right eye and even less hearing in his right ear, said to Brooks, "Seems like Mr. Burroughs don't want to talk to the likes of us."

Brooks narrowed his eyes and allowed the corners of his mouth to etch into a sneer.

"Thinks he's better'n everybody else. Don't make no matter. We've hit the mother lode. Getting paid to kill Frank

Gaffrey when I'd of done it for free. And it won't end there. That squaw'll be ours again and Jacob Riley's wife will be a widow."

Wildcat didn't hear a word Brooks said. He was busy finishing off what was left in the small jug he had attached to the rope around his neck.

Chapter 26

Gaffrey's last purchase at the General Store had been a two shot .32 caliber derringer. When they stopped mid-afternoon to water the horses, he presented the gun to Yellow Moon. "You were good with that knife, but this might prove more useful next time trouble comes."

Jacob added with a chuckle, "Yellow Moon, remind me not to make you mad. You know where to cut a man so he don't have to worry about siring no offspring."

Yellow Moon's eyes flashed. "John Brooks is not a man. He is an animal. If their souls could speak, his unborn children would thank me."

Jacob was surprised at the force of Yellow Moon's anger. "You're right about that. He ain't fit to be a human being, much less a husband or father to no children."

After making sure Yellow Moon understood how to load and fire the derringer, Gaffrey felt better about her being able to protect herself should something happen to him and Jacob. He felt relieved, but he knew there were no guarantees. Anything could happen to anybody at anytime. All he could do is try to make the odds favor them a little more.

They arrived at the cabin at the end of the day, a brilliant array of colors—orange, red, pink and purple—flooded the northern sky and signaled a big sky sunset. The men unloaded the supplies and tended the horses and wagon. Yellow Moon started a cook fire in the large stone hearth. She had missed this place even more than she thought she would. Filling the iron cook pot with the ingredients of their supper, she felt torn by her longing to see her people again and stay forever in this beautiful valley.

"Damn, if this place don't feel like home," Jacob exclaimed as he dropped an armload of firewood next to the hearth.

Yellow Moon looked up from the pot and smiled at Jacob. "Yes, it is a beautiful place. I missed the smell of it."

Gaffrey walked through the door with his saddlebag slung over his shoulder. "What's for supper?"

* * * *

Burroughs and his men moved out in the gray of a new morning's light. Burroughs led the way with Powder riding on his right and the two hired guns on his left. John Brooks had ridden ahead to look for the trail, leaving Wildcat passed out in the chuck wagon.

* * * *

So far, it had been a good spring. Well rested, he had found plenty to eat and was beginning to feel less cranky as he neared his full weight. Except for the newcomers, his valley was just the way it was supposed to be, peaceful. He had checked on them several times. The last time he observed their cabin it seemed they had left--which suited him just fine. They must have taken his warning to heart. However this morning, he had picked up another scent, an old memory, one that sent him into a rage unlike any other he had ever experienced. The men who had caused him untold suffering were back.

* * * *

John Brooks returned to camp sweating and excited. His eyes were bright and alert for the first time in many months.

After taking a long pull from the jug Wildcat offered him, he reported to Hart Burroughs. "I found them. I shorely did. They're about a half-day's ride from here. It won't be long now, Mr. Burroughs."

"That's good news," the rancher grunted. "You can take me and Powder in the morning to check things out."

"Well, Mr. Burroughs, I was thinking since you been so good to me'n Wildcat, why don't you just let us take care of them? It would shorely be our pleasure."

Burroughs rolled his eyes. "Let you and Haynes take care of them? Why the hell would I want to do that? As best as I can remember, the last time you tried to take care of them, they ended taking care of you! You two are lucky to be alive."

Powder smiled.

Wildcat chimed in, "If I hadn't got bushwhacked by that mad dog, things would've...."

"Shut-up," Brooks interrupted, giving Wildcat a look that almost made him pass out with fear. John Brooks managed to restrain himself. "Whatever you say Mr. Burroughs. You're the boss."

"That's right," Burroughs replied, "I am the boss and you'd be wise to remember that. After you show us the location, I'll pay you what you're due and you'll be free to leave. I'll even throw in the horses and some provisions."

"Whatever you say," Brooks mumbled as he walked away. As far as John Brooks was concerned, Hart Burroughs would have to take his revenge out on whatever was left of Gaffrey after he and Wildcat got through with him.

Chapter 27

Yellow Moon woke with a start. Although they occurred with less frequency, she still had nightmares from her time with the two trappers. Last night had been especially difficult. She got quietly out of her bed, wrapping her blanket around her. She peered out the cabin window into the early morning mist. She heard the sound of a black crow calling. Gaffrey had one of his spells last night, the first he had experienced in a long time. Fortunately, it passed quickly. She could hear Jacob stirring as she put on the coffee.

* * * *

Hart Burroughs had positioned his men carefully. The morning mist fit nicely with his plan, allowing Powder to set some explosives under the left corner of the barn. After placing a feed bag in the barn, Powder worked as quickly as possible. Liberty was snorting and stomping impatiently. One of the packhorses began whinnying. When the mists cleared, Burroughs would give the signal and Powder would set off the charge. According to his foreman, the explosion would be enough to eliminate any means of quick escape for Gaffrey and his friends.

* * * *

Gaffrey sat on the side of his bunk and rubbed his eyes.

"How's your head feelin'?" Jacob asked.

"Bit of a headache, but it's all right. Nothing a cup of hot coffee can't fix."

Yellow Moon handed him a cup of the steaming brew.

Jacob stoked the fire with an iron poker. "Yellow Moon heard the horses fussin' out in the barn. So I went and checked on them."

Gaffrey pressed the hot tin cup to his forehead. "What spooked them?"

"Can't rightly say," Jacob replied. "By the way, did you put a feedbag out last night?"

Gaffrey drank some of the coffee. "Don't think so. Probably should have. With the spell and all, I don't really remember."

"Yeah, me neither. Things got right hectic last night. You ain't had one of them fits in a long time."

Gaffrey stuck his cup out as Yellow Moon refilled it. "Not long enough to suit me."

Yellow Moon poured corn meal into a pot of boiling water suspended over the fire. "It wasn't as bad as in the past."

Gaffrey looked at her and nodded in agreement.

* * * *

Before Powder went to set the charges, he brought Brooks to Hart Burroughs' tent. Burroughs handed Brooks a leather pouch. "Here's the wages I promised you for finding Gaffrey. You can count it if you want to."

"No need," a sullen Brooks replied.

Burroughs pointed at the two horses hitched to a tether line. "Those two horses are packed with five days worth of provisions which should give you a good start to wherever you're headed next."

Brooks nodded.

"I want the two of you out of here before the shooting starts. That understood?"

"Understood." Brooks turned and walked away. Let him think what he wants to. It ain't over til I say it's over.

Burroughs had instructed Powder to take three of the ranch hands to a thicket of trees just north of the cabin and barn. The two hired guns and a half dozen other men spread out according to their instructions. They concealed themselves behind rocks and trees approximately a hundred yards facing the cabin.

When he was making final plans the previous night with Powder, he indicated that their best angle of attack was also the most vulnerable position. Sipping brandy from a silver flask, Burroughs offered Powder a cigar.

"No thanks, Mr. Burroughs."

"That's right. You're not a smoker. Wonder if Gaffrey smokes? No mind. You got the charges ready and the men clear on their firing positions?"

"Yes, Sir."

"Good, Powder, good," Burroughs replied, lighting a cigar and exhaling. "Unfortunately our best firing line is also their best shooting angle. We'll suffer some casualties, but that cabin won't be enough to protect them from our overall firepower."

"No, sir."

"I'll give that son of a bitch credit. He's a sly one, building the cabin backed up to the rock wall. That was a smart move."

"Yes sir, it was."

The two men shook hands. It was time. Burroughs was ready for Gaffrey's account to be settled. Burroughs himself was positioned less than a hundred yards south of the cabin with two of his men. Three additional gunmen lined the ridge above the barn, their rifles ready. Well out of range of the cabin, a single man tended the horses to the rear where the cook managed the chuck wagon.

Burroughs fingered his custom made hunting rifle, a gift from his son the last Christmas he was alive. He ran his hand gently over the smooth wood, remembering that morning. He could feel the anger rising in his throat and gripped the rifle tightly. Powder's instructions to the men were clear—after the explosion, lay down a withering field of gunfire on the cabin's occupants. Shoot to kill Riley or the Indian girl if they got in the way, but no one but Burroughs himself would shoot Gaffrey. Once Gaffrey was killed, his two friends were to be spared if they were still alive.

* * * *

Gaffrey and Jacob sipped their morning coffee while Yellow Moon stirred a pot of cornmeal and molasses. Gaffrey felt lucky that the spell had passed so quickly, leaving him only slightly weakened with a mild headache. He and Jacob would need all the strength they could muster to get the new cabin ready. Pouring Jacob and himself another cup of coffee, Gaffrey began to relax. He pondered Burroughs' next move. Burroughs would come looking for him, but probably not before he procured the services of some additional hired guns and one or two Indian scouts. And that would take at least a week.

Gaffrey was reaching for the bowl Yellow Moon held out when the explosives detonated with a deafening roar.

Chapter 28

Jacob jumped at the sound of the explosion, spilling hot coffee all over himself.

Yellow Moon dropped the bowl of mush on the floor.

Gaffrey reached for his rifle.

All hell broke loose. A third of the barn blew off. Pieces of wood and metal flew in every direction as the barn collapsed around screaming horses. Flying pieces of timber and debris slammed into the side of the cabin. A single chunk of rock crashed through one of the shutters. Jacob's horse was killed immediately and another was on the ground in the throes of death. Liberty and the two mules ran wild-eyed for the woods.

Burroughs' men held their fire as instructed. They were not to shoot until Gaffrey or one of the others showed themselves. Burroughs waited patiently. Justice was near.

Instinctively, Jacob grabbed his Winchester and rushed toward the barn. Gaffrey shouted for him to wait, but it was too late. He was out the door. A fuselage of gunfire greeted Jacob as he ran toward what was left of the barn. He was hit twice. One bullet passed through the fleshy part of his left thigh. Another bullet embedded itself just above his left elbow. Breathing heavily, Jacob curled up behind the buckboard. He tried to make himself as small a target as possible.

The gunfire subsided as Burroughs' men waited for his signal to resume. Burroughs was in no hurry. He had all the firepower. Let Gaffrey and his friends sweat a little before he gave the order to resume firing.

* * * *

The scent was getting stronger. His heart beat faster as he crashed through the underbrush. He held deep within him a lifetime of fury ready to burst forth into action.

* * * *

Gaffrey handed Yellow Moon a rifle and positioned her next to a shooting port near the front of the cabin. Her face was streaked with sweat. He could see both fear and resolve in her eyes. "Just do the best you can. Try to maintain a steady fire. Maybe it will at least divert some of the fire from Jacob. I'm going up on the roof where I can do some damage."

Yellow Moon nodded. "Be careful."

Gaffrey slipped through the hatch onto the roof. The mist was all but gone as he surveyed the surroundings through his field glasses. The gun smoke from Burroughs' men mixed with the mist still hanging above the cabin's roof.

Gaffrey squinted through the smoke and mist. What hampered his line of sight also hid him from the enemy's view. What he saw when he finally got a good look almost made him throw up. He had been outnumbered before, but this time he was completely surrounded. He would do what he could. The outcome was no longer up to him. It was Antietam all over again.

With a drop of the hand, Burroughs' men resumed firing at Jacob and the cabin.

John Brooks and Wildcat Haynes peered out from the cover of the forest.

"That's some fireworks show," Wildcat gleefully exclaimed, sloshing whiskey all over himself as he tried to drink and talk at the same time. "There may not be nothing left of Gaffrey or Yellow Moon 'fore it's over."

Brooks drank deeply from his jug and narrowed his eyes. "Gaffrey won't go down that easy. That other feller might not make it, but Gaffrey knows what he's doin'. We'll get a piece of him 'fore it's over."

* * * *

Although he could hear the sound of Yellow Moon's rifle below, Gaffrey chose to hold his fire for the time being. The mist was still too thick to maximize his accuracy. He knew he and Yellow Moon could escape through the cave, but that would mean abandoning Jacob. That was always the trouble with caring about people. If it was just himself, he could stay and fight or escape with nothing to lose. That was no longer possible. The fate of his two friends were tied to his own. He was responsible for them, a feeling that took away some of the edge that made him dangerous and unpredictable. He could feel the beginning of another dull headache.

Gaffrey wasn't much of praying man, but he closed his eyes, "Lord, please don't let my friends die. Help me protect them."

Chapter 29

Inside, one look on Gaffrey's face told Yellow Moon all she needed to know. She slipped the derringer into her waistband in the small of her back and her knife into her left sleeve. An open box of ammunition lay on the floor beside her. Neither said anything as Gaffrey returned to the roof with his Henry and two additional boxes of ammunition.

Drenched with sweat, Yellow Moon resumed firing.

The latest fuselage grazed the right side of Riley's face, causing him to hunker down even more behind the shelter of the overturned wagon. He got off an occasional wild shot, but could do little more. He had fashioned a tourniquet for his thigh wound. He did his best to block out the throbbing pain in his left arm. Things didn't look good. What little faith Jacob had left was in his friend, Gaffrey.

Burroughs had waited long enough. They weren't going to be flushed out that easily, although he knew as well as Gaffrey did, that time was on his side. He was beginning to grow impatient. He gave the signal. The roar of more than a dozen guns exploded repeatedly at the cabin and Jacob.

Yellow Moon hugged the floor as bullets whizzed around her. She gently sang her tribe's death chant. She couldn't help feeling the end was near. It wasn't what she wanted. But she could accept it as long as she was with Gaffrey.

As Gaffrey peeked over the edge of the roof, the mist had finally lifted enough for him to target some of the shooters. He eased the Henry into a good shooting position. Bracing himself, he slowly exhaled and gently squeezed the trigger. The Henry found its mark. The first two shooters he picked off were the hired guns. Never wear a black Stetson with a silver hatband to a pitched gun battle, he thought. Hired guns, particularly younger wannabes, tended to be cocky and not well versed in this type of shoot-out. They were more accustomed to the art of ambush, of shooting someone in the back. Moving back and forth along the roofline, he located other shooters. The accuracy of the Henry resulted in three more wounded ranch hands. Their cries of pain echoed through the gunfire.

By crawling along the cabin's roofline on his belly, Gaffrey remained largely undetected. With all the shooting, Burroughs' men couldn't be sure where the deadly return fire was coming from. They assumed that, except for Jacob, it was coming from the cabin's shooting ports. They didn't know about the secret hatch. With the help of the natural camouflage of trees surrounding the back of the cabin where it joined with the cave, they didn't recognize Gaffrey's location or vantage point. He tried to fire just after and during the firing from Jacob and Yellow Moon so his gun smoke would less likely be noticed.

When Hart Burroughs signaled his men to stop shooting for a second time, Jacob took stock of his wounds. Touching the right side of his face, he could feel that the blood had already crusted. His leg was another matter. Even with the tourniquet, the wound in his thigh was still bleeding profusely. He felt dizzy. If he could crawl to the woodpile next to the stand of trees near the rear of the cabin, he would have a good chance to make it inside. Gaffrey's gunfire came regularly from the roof so Jacob knew Gaffrey was all right. He wondered how Yellow Moon was doing. He watched for her fire from the gun ports. Since the last volley from Burroughs' men, he hadn't seen her return fire. He prayed she was all right.

Jacob muttered, "I love you Naomi", took a deep breath and half ran, half stumbled toward the safety of the cabin.

Burroughs had signaled another cease-fire to re-supply his men.

Gaffrey watched Jacob make his way across the yard. He lay ready to pick off anyone who fired at his friend.

Yellow Moon watched from her window too. Her gun tip stationed part way out the portal, followed Jacob's progression across the yard. She said a quick prayer that Burroughs' men wouldn't spot him. Suddenly, fifteen feet from safety, one of Powder Falen's bullets found its mark. Jacob pitched forward, face first, grabbing his left shoulder. Yellow Moon dropped her rifle and sprinted from the cabin to the aid of her fallen friend.

A fresh volley of gunfire brought Yellow Moon to her knees. Clutching her right arm, she crawled to her wounded friend and covered him with her body.

Laying his Henry down, Gaffrey stood up, "Burroughs! Let the girl and Jacob live."

Burroughs called for the shooting to cease. All fell silent, with only the moans and cries of the wounded still audible. Burroughs shouted, "Come out in front of the cabin where I can see you."

* * * *

Wildcat and Brooks watched the drama unfold before them. Slapping his right leg, Wildcat guffawed, "This is shore enough entertainin'. This is about better'n anything I ever seen. Wonder what's gonna happen next?"

John Brooks glared at him. "Shut your fool mouth. Come with me and you'll see."

* * * *

Gaffrey climbed down through the roof's hatch. He passed through the cabin, taking one last look as he did. He took a deep breath before stepping outside. Ten yards to his right, Yellow Moon, although bleeding from the wound in her right arm, was bending over Jacob and speaking in low soothing tones as a mother would to her child. Burroughs stood on the large elevated rock seventy-five yards to Gaffrey's left.

Gaffrey clenched his fists at his sides and walked out in the open to face his enemy.

"Judgment day has come, Gaffrey. You took my son's life and now I'm going to take yours." Burroughs raised his rifle and took aim.

Brooks appeared unexpectedly from the nearby shadow of the woods with Wildcat following a short distance behind him. Brooks grabbed Yellow Moon and dragged her by her hair to a safe distance from where Gaffrey stood.

Her knife had dropped from her sleeve. It lay in the dirt next to Jacob who was barely conscious. Hart Burroughs lowered his rifle and looked on incredulously.

"Well, hello again Mr. Burroughs," Brooks said with a sneer.

"What the hell are you doing here, Brooks? You got your wages. I told you and your sidekick to be on your way."

Brooks spat, "You ain't the only person who's due some justice. I got me some satisfaction coming too."

Yellow Moon struggled to get at the derringer. She tried to twist around in Brooks' grasp. He pulled her head further back in response. On her knees with her head bent backward toward the ground, she stretched her left arm in one last desperate attempt to reach the derringer. She didn't want to die, especially at the hand of John Brooks.

Brooks spotted the derringer as her fingers closed around it. He kicked it out of her hand. He tightened his chokehold on Yellow Moon with his other hand, causing her to gasp for breath. For a moment, Gaffrey thought she was going to lose consciousness.

"Not just yet squaw. Soon, but not just yet," Brooks said, glaring at Gaffrey. Turning his attention back to Burroughs, Brooks made his intentions clear. "The last thing I want this scumsucker to see before your bullet takes his life is me taking the life of the squaw he stole from me. Don't nobody take what's mine."

"That's right. You tell 'em Big John," echoed Wildcat, waving his arms in a drunken stupor.

Burroughs said nothing for a moment. He gazed thoughtfully at the strange sight before him. He slowly raised his rifle and sighted it. In that millisecond, Gaffrey and Yellow Moon's eyes met and held each other as Burroughs cocked the rifle.

Chapter 30

Yellow Moon moved slightly. Brooks tightened his grip again. The blade of his knife flicked into the skin on Yellow Moon's neck. A gentle stream of blood seeped downward, staining her deerskin tunic.

Gaffrey watched the thin red line of blood trickle down her neck and waited for the bullet with his name on it. He had never felt as helpless as he did now.

The blast from Burroughs' rifle echoed like a cannon throughout the valley. It seemed as though time stood still as the large caliber bullet sped across the open ground toward its intended target.

It tore a hole the size of a silver dollar in John Brooks' stomach. The force propelled him backwards. He flew through the air and landed flat on his back. Everyone stood transfixed as Brooks slowly sat up and peered incredulously down at the blood gushing between his fingers. He grunted once and fell face first on the ground, his life's blood draining into the rich Montana dirt.

Gaffrey and Yellow Moon looked at each other in amazement. Gaffrey turned his attention to Hart Burroughs. Neither man spoke as their eyes met.

Burroughs fingered his rifle. Suddenly he leaned down

and handed the rifle to a ranch hand. He whispered something to him and motioned to the rear. As he climbed off the rock, another cowboy rode up with his horse.

Burroughs mounted his horse and turned back toward Gaffrey for one last look. The pain and anger was still there, but there was something else. He pulled a cigar from his coat, lit it and rode off in a cloud of dust.

Gaffrey couldn't believe what had just taken place. His legs were shaking and he was having difficulty breathing. In a matter of minutes, the remaining gunmen disappeared. Gaffrey stood there watching the dust of their horses dissipate.

Tears streamed down Yellow Moon's face.

After several moments of stunned silence, they bent to examine Jacob. Gently they moved him inside the cabin. Yellow Moon put on a kettle of water to boil. Gaffrey cut Jacob's shirt and pants away from his wounds.

Yellow Moon tried to steady herself, resting her head against the cabin wall as Gaffrey attended to Jacob. Suddenly, they heard a rider approach and call Gaffrey's name. Had Burroughs changed his mind? Gaffrey took a breath and opened the door enough to see Powder Falen stopping his horse in front of the porch. Gaffrey stepped outside, rifle in hand. It was aimed directly at Powder Falen's chest.

"Mr. Burroughs said to bring this horse and supplies to you. There's bandages, some lineament and food." Powder tipped his hat. His horse reared slightly as he reined it backward and rode away.

Frank shook his head in weary amazement.

Chapter 31

Wildcat Haynes' pickled brain had difficulty processing what had taken place. His first impression was that Hart Burroughs was the worst shot he had ever come across when he missed Gaffrey at such close range. Then he realized that Burroughs had intentionally killed Brooks.

Terrified, Wildcat broke and ran for the forest, certain that he'd be next. He ran wildly through the woods, imagining both Gaffrey and Burroughs were in hot pursuit. The dense underbrush scratched his face. He fell twice, the second time rolling down a rocky twelve-foot embankment. Getting to his feet, he bent and clutched his knees to catch his breath. Wildcat listened for the sounds of his pursuers, but all he could hear was his own heavy breathing.

As the fog in his brain began to clear, he remembered where he and Brooks had hidden the twenty five-dollar gold pieces Hart Burroughs had paid them. He relaxed a little. Taking what was left of the half-pint of whiskey out of his coat pocket, he pulled out the cork with the few good teeth he had left and spit it out. He took a long pull from the bottle and things began to look a little better as far as Wildcat was concerned.

* * * *

Jacob groaned as Gaffrey tried to stabilize his shattered shoulder. Yellow Moon had cleaned and bandaged Jacob's thigh wound. Exhausted, she sat on the floor leaning back against the bed Jacob lay in.

"His left arm is a mess," Gaffrey said as much to himself as to Yellow Moon. "Looks like the bullet that passed through his forearm may have nicked a bone. I don't know whether his shoulder will heal or not. All I can do is secure his left arm to his chest with bandages."

"The bullet passed through his thigh cleanly. It should heal," Yellow Moon said quietly as she closed her eyes.

Gaffrey looked down at her. "What about your arm?"

"It will heal," she replied, without opening her eyes.

Gaffrey carefully picked up Yellow Moon and carried her to her bed. She moaned softly as he tenderly cleaned and bandaged her arm. Then sleep overtook her.

* * * *

Wildcat Haynes retraced his steps toward the large oak next to a small stream. Along the way, he tried to use what small portion of his brain that still functioned to come up with a plan for his future.

"Lordy, Lordy Big John what did they do to you? They shot you dead, that's what they did. Yesirree, they shorely did. And that means we ain't partners no more cause Wildcat can't be partners with no dead man. He shorely can't. And since we ain't partners no more, them twenty five-dollar gold pieces goes to yours truly. Yesirree, they shorely do."

Wildcat reached into a hollow place in the old oak tree. He pulled out the sack of coins as well as the three rifles he and Brooks had stolen from the supply wagon. Bending over the coins and counting them one more time, he heard the bushes behind him move.

* * * *

Fighting overwhelming weariness, Gaffrey stared out the window into the coming evening. Jacob was snoring, compliments of a half jug of whiskey. Yellow Moon dozed in a fitful sleep. Walking out on the porch, Gaffrey heard Liberty's familiar snort as he led the two mules toward the cabin.

* * * *

Grabbing one of the rifles, Wildcat turned toward the sound behind him. What he saw caused his one good eye to almost bulge out of its socket. Towering before him was the largest bear he had ever seen. Frozen, Wildcat dropped the rifle. He stared upwards in horror as the giant grizzly thundered its rage.

It was the last sight Wildcat's one good eye would ever see.

* * * *

He hadn't forgotten what they did to his Mother. Only a cub, he had hidden nearby when they killed her. He had cried over her mutilated corpse for days. He remembered the pain and the ones who caused it. The trappers' smell was filed away in his memory. It came alive the day they returned to his valley.

* * * *

On the evening of the shooting, Gaffrey and Yellow Moon awoke, startled by a strange sound. They thought they heard someone screaming deep in the forest. Whatever it was, they had been too tired and exhausted to investigate.

Years later, a Shoshone hunting party came upon a strange sight at the base of a giant oak—the remains of a human skeleton that suggested the arms and legs had been literally pulled out of their sockets. Interspersed with the bones were twenty five-dollar gold pieces. High above the pile of bones, a pulverized human skull hung, anchored by a broken branch protruding through one of the eye sockets. Just below the skull, the trunk of the tree bore a series of massive claw marks.

Chapter 32

It had been almost three weeks since the shoot-out with Burroughs and his men. Jacob and Yellow Moon nursed their wounds and rested. Gaffrey repaired the barn and cleaned up the place as best he could by himself. He used Liberty and the pack mules to drag the two dead horses to a nearby ravine where he covered the bodies with rocks.

Other than a few scrapes, Gaffrey had emerged from the confrontation largely unscathed. Yellow Moon's wound to her left arm was healing quickly. Brook's knife had not cut too deeply into her neck although there would be a small permanent scar.

Jacob was another matter. The first ten days were touch and go as his body fought infection. Gaffrey had to lance his thigh twice to let some of the poison drain out. Yellow Moon prepared a poultice of herbs and applied them to his shoulder. She sat by Jacob's bedside each of the ten nights and bathed his fevered brow with cool spring water, talking to him in a soft, comforting voice.

At the end of the second week, Jacob's fever broke and he began to heal more rapidly. Although his shoulder continued to cause him a great deal of pain, by the end of the third week, some of the old fire started to return to Jacob Riley. "If I didn't know better, I'd say I'm in about as bad a shape as you were when the Medicine Bear got hold of you."

"I'd have to agree with you on that point," Gaffrey replied as he poured Jacob a fresh cup of coffee. Gaffrey held up a bottle of whiskey, "You want a little of this in it to help with the pain?"

"Don't mind if I do," Jacob quickly replied.

Gaffrey handed his friend the cup and sat down on the end of Jacob's bed. Leaning back against the cabin wall, he filled and lit his briar. The two men sat silently, watching Yellow Moon prepare the evening meal with her left arm in a sling. Gaffrey had tried to help her with supper, but she would have none of it. Jacob drifted off to sleep while Gaffrey continued looking at Yellow Moon.

He thought about how she'd changed from the emaciated ghost of a girl to the beautiful woman she was now. Her long, dark hair had a sheen which reflected the firelight from the hearth. Her hair complimented her soulful eyes that, depending on the light, could look either gray or green.

Suddenly she became aware of his gaze and turned toward him. That look never ceased to unsettle him a little. He wondered if she was aware of her affect on him. It was as though she could see into the innermost part of him—his struggles, the feelings he was unsure of—ones that had remained dormant, buried deep within him for many years.

There she was, squatting near the fire, looking into him with a certainty and completeness that spoke of a deep and trusting love. There was confidence and strength in her gaze that was borne of a love that was unconditional. He knew then that whether they were together or apart, Yellow Moon would love him for the rest of her life. Did she choose to love Gaffrey or did love itself make the choice? Gaffrey didn't know or care. All he knew for certain was that his heart was pounding in his chest. He wondered if she could hear it.

They looked at each other in silence, she with her gift and he with his need. Yellow Moon crossed the room. She reached out and touched his face. "It will be all right. Whatever happens will be all right."

Gaffrey felt himself being drawn into the very heart of Yellow Moon. Her heart was big enough and her love strong enough to surround his loneliness. Her gaze washed over him like soft moonlight as he began to let go of his fear. And suddenly as he looked deeper into her eyes, he saw something else--something that both startled him and filled him with joy. It was the beauty of a Montana summer morning. Gaffrey's eyes began to hurt. He rubbed them and realized tears were streaming down his cheeks. After Antietam, he thought he would never cry again. But the vision in Yellow Moon's eyes told him that he had found the place that he was looking for. Wherever she was, was where he wanted to be. Love had finally found Frank Gaffrey and he would never be the same again.

Chapter 33

It had been a truly amazing year. Like so much of living, Gaffrey could never tell what was around the next curve of the road.

They had lived to see another Christmas Eve. He stood on the front porch of the cabin they'd worked so hard to build. He puffed on his pipe and watched the rings of smoke waft to the ceiling.

Turning his head toward the laughter and music inside, he couldn't help but smile and reflect upon his good fortune. He still marveled at Hart Burroughs sparing his life. Just as he and the recovering Jacob were pondering how they would ever be able to build a home for his family, who showed up but Naomi and the children. They drove a wagon loaded with supplies. Elroy Foster and Gene Hill rode behind them with the live-stock. Sheriff Hill had left Alec Mason, his chief deputy, in charge and had accompanied Naomi and the children to make sure that they arrived safely and to help with the construction.

Apparently, Powder Falen, on orders from Burroughs, had shown up one morning on Naomi's doorstep and handed her a map to the cabin. He had informed her that Jacob was wounded and would need some seeing after.

Gaffrey laughed, remembering what Naomi had said to Elroy and the Sheriff after she got Powder's news. "I'm going to my Jacob through hell and high water if need be. The devil himself better not get in my way."

No matter how long he lived, Gaffrey would never understand why at the last moment, Hart Burroughs had a change of heart. Maybe Yellow Moon was right when she said Burroughs changed his mind in the moment he realized that his gun also controlled John Brooks' knife. That in killing Gaffrey, his spirit would be bound forever with Brooks in killing her. Yellow Moon believed in the end, Hart Burroughs chose to let the good in him become stronger than his fear and grief. Now, she believed, his heart would come alive again. Gaffrey hoped she was right.

After a string of hard times, good fortune continued to shine on them. Jacob and Naomi's cabin had gone up ahead of schedule. Gaffrey watched Naomi in awe. She was everywhere—cooking, hammering, sawing, and whatever else needed doing. Her cheerfulness was infectious and her strength and endurance could just about match his and Jacob's. After Sheriff Hill had departed, Gaffrey, Elroy, Jacob, and Jacob's son, Elijah spent the second half of summer hunting and curing meat for the winter. They made one last trip to Morristown in the waning days of late summer for winter supplies and a special occasion. Elroy stayed behind to care for the animals.

Gaffrey smiled again, this time more broadly, as he remembered that trip. Although it didn't seem to matter much to Yellow Moon and he figured it probably seemed odd to the townspeople of Morristown, he and Yellow Moon were married by Judge Hugh Bell. She wore a new calico dress and put her hair up just to oblige Naomi and the photographer Jacob had hired for the occasion. She surely did look pretty all dressed up, but she looked just as beautiful dressed in deer-skin.

He hadn't contacted Mary Simpson. There didn't seem to be much point. Gaffrey realized that given a different place and time, different choices might have been made. He had been both surprised and pleased when Bessie had visited him while they were in town. She carried a message from Mary.

Dear Frank:
Please accept my best wishes on your marriage
and the white linen table cloth as a wedding present to
the two of you.
Best,
Mary

Gaffrey had deeply disappointed her, but he knew just as well that she was strong and had a good heart. He hoped she would find happiness. If anyone deserved it, she did. Yes, it had been quite a year and he was grateful.

"Frank, what are you doing out here?" Yellow Moon asked softly as she held up the oil lantern to see her way next to him.

Gaffrey took the lantern and blew it out. Setting it down on the front porch rail, he moved behind Yellow Moon and encircled her with his arms, feeling her growing belly which promised new life in the spring.

She leaned back against him, placing her hands on top of his.

"I was out here looking at all those stars and wondering about things—wondering about our good fortune," he said.

"Yes," Yellow Moon responded, "it is a beautiful sight."

"And I guess, maybe, I was dreaming a little too."

Yellow Moon turned her face toward his and kissed him lightly. "Sometimes dreams come true."

ABOUT THE AUTHOR

M.M. Braswell is a writing team.

Michael Braswell is a former prison psychologist and teacher at East Tennessee State University in Criminal Justice. His publications include "Remembering Peleliu and other World War II stories", "Long Road Home: The Trials and Tribulations of a Confederate Soldier," a novel he coauthored with Richard Zevitz and "Stray Dogs," a short story collection he coauthored with Scott Braswell.

Mark Braswell is a former probation officer who currently works as a Security Supervisor for a college.